"Do You Want To Be Kissed?" He Asked.

"I've been, thanks," she said, though he thought he heard growing excitement in her voice.

"Oh, I see," he said, his voice very low. "Once was enough, was it?"

She nodded. "Just about. I'll admit I gave it a few more tries, but the result was the same."

"You know what that tells me?" He had her shoulders in hand. He knew he was crossing the line, but it was too late to turn around now. "It's been much too long since you've tried it."

She stared up at him, fascinated by how full and soft his lips looked all of a sudden, by how fast her heart was beating. "Do you really think so?" she said faintly.

"Yes, I do," he murmured as he bent to find her mouth with his.

Dear Reader,

Cowboys and cops…sexy men with a swagger…just the kind of guys to make your head turn. *That's* what we've got for you this month in Silhouette Desire.

The romance begins when Taggart Jones meets his match in Anne McAllister's wonderful MAN OF THE MONTH, *The Cowboy and the Kid*. This is the latest in her captivating CODE OF THE WEST miniseries. And the fun continues with Mitch Harper in *A Gift for Baby*, the next book in Raye Morgan's THE BABY SHOWER series.

Cindy Gerard has created a dynamic hero in the *very* masculine form of J. D. Hazzard in *The Bride Wore Blue*, book #1 in the NORTHERN LIGHTS BRIDES series. And if rugged rascals are your favorite, don't miss Jake Spencer in Dixie Browning's *The Baby Notion*, which is book #1 of DADDY KNOWS LAST, Silhouette's new cross-line continuity. (Next month, look for Helen R. Myers's *Baby in a Basket* as DADDY KNOWS LAST continues in Silhouette Romance!)

Gavin Cantrell is sure to weaken your knees in *Gavin's Child* by Caroline Cross, part of the delightful BACHELORS AND BABIES promotion. And Jackie Merritt—along with hero Duke Sheridan—kicks off her MADE IN MONTANA series with *Montana Fever*.

Heroes to fall in love with—and love scenes that will make your toes curl. That's what Silhouette Desire is all about. Until next month—enjoy!

All the best,

Lucia Macro

Senior Editor

Please address questions and book requests to:
Silhouette Reader Service
U.S.: 3010 Walden Ave., P.O. Box 1325, Buffalo, NY 14269
Canadian: P.O. Box 609, Fort Erie, Ont. L2A 5X3

RAYE
MORGAN
A GIFT FOR BABY

SILHOUETTE *Desire*

Published by Silhouette Books

America's Publisher of Contemporary Romance

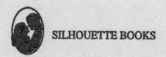

SILHOUETTE BOOKS

ISBN 0-373-76010-8

A GIFT FOR BABY

Copyright © 1996 by Helen Conrad

Books by Raye Morgan

Silhouette Desire

Embers of the Sun #52
Summer Wind #101
Crystal Blue Horizon #141
A Lucky Streak #393
Husband for Hire #434
Too Many Babies #543
Ladies' Man #562
In a Marrying Mood #623
Baby Aboard #673
Almost a Bride #717
The Bachelor #768
Caution: Charm at Work #807
Yesterday's Outlaw #836
The Daddy Due Date #843
Babies on the Doorstep #886
Sorry, the Bride Has Escaped #892
*Baby Dreams #997
*A Gift for Baby #1010

*The Baby Shower

Silhouette Romance

Roses Never Fade #427

RAYE MORGAN

favors settings in the West, which is where she has spent most of her life. She admits to a penchant for Western heroes, believing that whether he's a rugged outdoorsman or a smooth city sophisticate, he tends to have a streak of wildness that the romantic heroine can't resist taming. She's been married to one of those Western men for twenty years and is busy raising four more in her Southern California home.

The Invitation

"**H**mm, pretty nice fit on that pair of jeans," Hailey Kingston thought idly as she glanced over the top of her sunglasses at the ranch hand walking by the pool. Then she stopped herself, appalled.

Good grief—had she come to this? Was she really so bored that she'd sunk to checking out the attributes of the local cowboys? There had to be something else to occupy her mind. Had to be.

Groaning, she stretched back on the chaise lounge and turned her face up to the sun, completely oblivious to the effect she was having on those very same cowboys. That was the way it always was. She just didn't care. She could walk around in a bikini as though it were a sweat suit, completely unconscious of the picture she made. Hailey Kingston was, in many ways, as natural as a child.

She wore her honey blond hair haphazardly, shoulder length and untamed. She seldom used makeup, and when she did, it was nothing more than a slash of pearly pink lipstick against her smooth, tanned skin. She was drop-dead gorgeous, and she couldn't help it. It was her blessing; it was her curse.

But it didn't mean much out here in the middle of nowhere. There was no one to see her but the two tiresome ex-cops who'd been sent to watch her every move, and the ranch hands and they'd been warned to stay away from her. At first, it had all seemed deliciously peaceful and serene, but after three weeks, it was just plain boring.

She heard the sound of boots scuffing along the gravel pathway and she turned, feeling defensive, to find one of the cowboys coming toward her, a shy grin on his young face. She frowned and waited until he reached where she was lounging, then asked, "May I help you?"

"Uh…" He held out a courier's packet awkwardly. "Up at the house, they told me to bring you this."

Lifting her sunglasses, she stared at his offering. "What is it?"

"I think it's your mail, miss."

"Mail!" She jumped up and took the bag from him greedily. Her quick thank-you was laced with a smile that made him gape, but she hardly noticed. News from the outside. Hallelujah. Maybe it was a letter from her father saying that this long nightmare was finally over and she could go home. He was the only one who knew where she was, the only one whose letters she was allowed to get.

But it wasn't from her father at all. What she found inside the packet was a pink envelope that smelled like…she gave a sniff. Baby powder. How in the world had this made its way through to her?

She knew they were holding back her letters. They didn't want her to have any contact with the outside world at all for fear someone would find out where she was. And yet, this little pink envelope had gotten through. This was her lucky day. It was bound to be an invitation to something. She ripped it open eagerly and pulled out a card shaped like a duck, wearing a silky satin bow and a silly smile.

A baby shower! She flipped open the card and read the details inside, along with a personal note at the bottom.

"Hailey, it's me! Can you believe it? You have to come and help me celebrate. No RSVP needed, because I know you'll be here!"

Hailey laughed softly. So, Sara was going to have a baby. "Oh, how wonderful," she said, sighing.

"What's that, ma'am?" The cowboy had been taking his time sauntering away, and when she spoke, he stopped and looked back hopefully.

"Uh, nothing," she said, nodding at him, then lifting her chin coolly. Tommy—wasn't that the name she'd heard him called? She was always careful not to give them false hope. It was best to let on right away that she had absolutely no interest in making friends. She'd learned young that her beauty could be a danger to everyone involved. He looked suitably abashed and she felt a twinge of remorse, but she knew better than to act on it. Best to let him think she was a snob. That would keep him at the distance that had to be maintained. He turned and went on his way, and she sighed.

Leaning down, she groped in her purse, found her wallet and opened it to the pictures. The wallet fell open naturally to a snapshot of the four young women, and she smiled at it.

There they were, the Fab Four—she and her three roommates in college. She'd carried that picture with her for eight years, and whenever things got a little too glum, she'd pull it out and remember the good times they'd had together.

Sara was going to be the first to have a baby, and maybe the only one, the way things were going. Hailey had talked to Cami Bishop, one of the foursome, on the telephone only a few months before, and Cami had more or less conceded defeat. She'd said she wasn't even looking for the "right man" any longer. She'd decided that illusive person was a member of a race that was now extinct. "Only a few fossils left," she'd joked, "to remind us of what we're missing."

Her other roomie, J. J. MacKenzie, was too full of ambition and in a career that demanded every ounce of strength. She didn't have time to think about babies. And Hailey herself—well, she had realized long ago that she would never be able to trust a man enough to build a lasting relationship. That was just the way it was.

But Sara—yes, they'd always known she would do it. Sara had come from the most perfect family and married someone who was, by all accounts, the most perfect man. And now she would have the perfect baby. It had been in the cards all along.

"Great," Hailey said softly, smiling a dreamy smile. "Good for her. Let her have a perfect baby. And let her have a perfect baby shower, too."

She pressed the invitation to her chest and looked around as though to guard it from prying eyes. "Oh yes, Sara. I will get to your shower," she whispered under her breath. "Somehow, someway, I will escape and get to you."

One

"Hey, Mitch. Look at that. It's the Ice Princess, come into town." The tall, handsome cowboy rapped his knuckles against the glass of the telephone booth to get his friend's attention. "Whachya say we go over and make ourselves helpful?"

Mitch Harper turned in the tiny booth, with the receiver still against his ear, more annoyed at the interruption from Larry than interested in seeing Hailey Kingston emerge from her low-slung sports car. Glancing at her, he shrugged and gestured his disinterest.

"I'm on the phone," he told Larry. "I'll be out in a minute."

Larry nodded good-naturedly and started across the street toward where Hailey stood adjusting a scarf she'd worn over her hair in the open car. Mitch watched her for a moment, his eyes narrowing, then his gaze focused on a pair of brightly attired men getting out of a gray sedan half a block away, and he shook his head, going back to his call.

"You really ought to do something about those two ex-cops they've got covering her," he said softly into the receiver. "They stick out like sore thumbs."

"Aren't they dressed for the area?" asked the gruff voice on the other end of the line.

"Sure. Circa 1950. They look like Roy Rogers and Dale Evans."

There was a pause. "Aren't they both guys?"

"Yup."

"Oh." The man on the line gave a snort of quick laughter. "I'll say something to the surveillance coordinator." He snickered again. "They don't suspect you, do they?"

"Those two?" Mitch smiled. "They don't have a clue. They think I'm a cowboy, just like everyone else does. Just another ranch hand."

"Good. I thought you would fit in pretty easily."

"Don't worry about me. I grew up not far from here. I know the area."

"But do they know you?"

"No. Not in this end of the valley."

"Good. Be careful." His voice got more businesslike. "Got anything for me?" he asked.

"Not yet," Mitch replied. "She's barely left the side of the pool for the past four days." He glanced across the street at where Hailey Kingston was still talking to Larry. As he watched, she began to walk into the store, and he had to admit, her walk had something to it, something a man couldn't ignore. Good thing he wasn't affected by things like that.

Yeah, right. Pulling himself together, he returned to his call. "If she's got anything inside that pretty head besides fluff, she's pretty good at hiding it."

"Don't underestimate her. She's the apple of her daddy's eye. If he's told anyone where the money is, it'll be her."

Mitch shook his head and his mouth turned down at the corners. The signs were not auspicious as far as he was concerned. "If she knows anything, she's a great bluffer."

"Hey, the best of them always seem innocent. Just keep an eye on her and give me a call if she does anything suspicious."

"Like booking a cruise or buying a diamond?"

"Like that, and any number of other things."

"You got it. And hey, Donagan." A smile crept into Mitch's voice. "Next assignment is back in the real world again—you got that? No more baby-sitting jobs."

"Hey, the next suicide mission is yours, Harper. You got my word on it."

After an exchange of friendly obscenities, Mitch rang off and made his way out of the booth, starting across the street toward where Larry was attempting to charm the lovely young woman in the sky blue jumper whose blond hair tumbled about her shoulders like surf on a rocky shore.

There was no doubt she was beautiful, and he was only human. But despite the reluctant admiration he couldn't help but have for her looks, he had nothing but contempt for everything else about her. The virtuous act didn't fool him for a moment. He'd been on a lot of these cases over the years, and it was his experience that these women were usually into things up to their delicately trimmed eyebrows, no matter how much innocence they pretended.

He hung back a bit, not wanting to draw attention his way. He'd decided not to get to know her from the start. Each job was unique. In some cases, the closer you got, the more you learned about the subject of the investigation. In others, it paid to stay back as an anonymous observer. That was the way he'd been playing it so far. Of course, it hadn't paid off with much information as yet, had it? Still, his instincts told him to keep his distance. He would just as soon she didn't notice him at all.

But he realized, with a wry twinge of humor, that he needn't have bothered to worry in this instance. Hailey Kingston's attention was focused fully on Larry Bartelli's handsome face as he helped her with the packages she was picking up at the local dress shop.

"Thank you," she told him as he stowed the parcels away in the boot of her foreign car. "I appreciate the help."

"My pleasure," Larry responded with a smile that he obviously hoped exuded raw seductive appeal. "Anytime you need me, you just call. I'm at your service."

"How comforting," she said after a pause. She reached into her purse. "Here, let me give you something for..."

"Oh, no, ma'am." Larry waved away her offer. "I don't need money. You can pay me back with just one of your pretty smiles. That's all I need."

She looked up at him and laughed softly. "If feminine smiles were really worth something, I have a feeling you'd be rich," she told him.

"Oh, no, Miss Kingston," he insisted earnestly. "Your smile is the only one that means anything to me."

She laughed again, tucking her purse under her arm. For just a moment, she glanced at Mitch, but he had his Stetson pushed down low over his eyes, and she didn't seem to see anything there worth lingering over.

"You're a lucky man, cowboy," she said, regarding Larry again with her head cocked to the side. "To be happy with such a simple gesture." She gave him a quick grin. "Especially since that's all you're ever going to get from me," she noted dryly under her breath. As she spoke, her two bodyguards approached the car, one walking with an exaggerated swagger, the other with a scowl.

"Move along, boys," the swaggerer barked at the two cowboys. "You know you're not supposed to bother Miss Kingston."

"No fraternization. That's the rules," the scowler added for good measure.

"It's all right," she said, turning to give them both a winning smile. "I asked for help. It's my fault."

The swaggerer looked aghast. "But *we're* here to help you, Miss Kingston. That's what they set up through the D.A.'s office. We're always here."

"Yes, I know." Her dry tone belied her feelings on the matter, and for a split second, her gaze met Mitch's and he saw the frustration in her eyes. But before he had time to connect with her look, she'd already turned and was sliding behind the wheel of her small car. Identical looks of panic crossed the faces of the two guards and they ran for their gray sedan. It was obvious they were afraid of losing her.

"She's ditched them before, I'll wager," Mitch muttered to himself with a smile as they roared off, chasing her dust.

But Larry wasn't listening. Sidling up to his friend, he clapped him on the back with a hearty pat. "Hey, she loves me," he announced happily.

If Larry had been looking, he might have noticed that the twist to Mitch's wide, hard mouth held more than a hint of sarcasm. "Is that right?"

"Yeah, can't you tell? Didn't you see the way she looked at me? She's crazy about me."

Mitch turned back toward the truck where they'd left it parked down the street a half block.

"Lucky you," he said dismissively. "But in the meantime, we've got things to do. We've still got to stop in and see the vet about those vitamins for that pregnant mare."

Larry fell into step beside him, his eyes sparkling from the encounter with Hailey. "She's gorgeous, isn't she? On a scale of one to ten, I'd give her a twenty. What do you think?"

Mitch was beginning to lose interest in the subject. "Personally, I'd give her a pass," he said shortly.

"You know what's wrong with you?" Larry babbled on happily. "You've got no romance in your soul."

Mitch nodded, in complete agreement on that score, and proud of it. He glanced at Larry. "And you've got no brain in your head if you think the powers that be are going to let you get anywhere near that woman."

Larry's smile was still just as broad. "Don't worry, pal. Love will find a way."

Mitch grunted a noncommittal sound and turned back toward the truck.

"Hey, man," Larry insisted, as though he felt he had to prove something to his companion. "I've got a knack with the girls, pal. They go for me in a big way."

Mitch gave him a pitying look. "Yes, I can tell girls like you a lot." He coughed carefully. "You might have a little more of a problem with real women, however," he murmured.

"Huh?" Larry frowned. "What does that mean?"

Mitch shrugged. "Never mind. Let's get out of here." He pulled open the door of the truck, ready to climb behind the wheel, but Larry couldn't let the subject go.

"Ah, you're just jealous," he ribbed as they got in and Mitch started the engine. "I know females. She's dreaming about me right now."

Maybe he was right, Mitch thought rather grumpily as they drove toward the office of the veterinarian. After all, he hadn't seen much evidence that she was much more than the bubbleheaded type who would go for a lightweight like Larry. And if she was dreaming about him, she probably deserved the fate that lay in wait for her. He certainly would do nothing to intervene. He just wanted to get this job over with and go back to something with a little more substance than this boring stint of surveillance.

"You're probably right," he muttered to Larry, to quiet him down. "You're probably right."

But Larry was wrong. Hailey's thoughts, as she drove toward the ranch, were a thousand miles away. They were centered somewhere outside of Denver at the moment.

"I could just keep driving," she was whispering to herself. "I could just go and go until dark." Looking in her rearview mirror, she could tell her bodyguards hadn't caught up with her dust trail as yet. "I could take a side road and lose them in minutes. No one would ever catch me."

But she laughed ruefully, knowing it was only a fantasy. She'd promised her father that she would stay put, and that was what she was going to have to do, no matter how agonizingly boring it became.

The first two weeks hadn't been too bad. She'd spent a lot of time catching up on her reading and her sleeping and her sunbathing. But now time was dragging, lengthening before her eyes, and she desperately needed something new to do.

She'd come here reluctantly. "Daddy," she'd insisted when her father had first brought it up. "I can handle myself. I've lived in the big city for too many years to be scared off because some sleazy mob guy is on my tail."

"It's more than that, sugar," he'd told her, shaking his shaggy white head of hair. "Much more. If someone got hold of you, they could buy my silence in a minute, and they're going to know it."

"Oh, Daddy." She loved the man so much. Ever since she'd lost her mother when she was entering her teen years, she'd depended on him in ways her friends never seemed to depend on their fathers. He was her confidante, her staunchest supporter, her buddy, her rock in a sea of uncertainty. The fact that he'd disappointed her in major ways in the past didn't matter. Her love went beyond that. She looked at his handsome, aging face and sighed. "Oh, Daddy," she said again softly.

"I mean it, honey. These guys play rough."

By now it was a foregone conclusion. Of course she was going to do as he asked. But she didn't tell him yet. Instead she played for time. "But . . . how did you get involved with these people in the first place?" she asked him.

"Doing business, sugar. My restaurants have been three of the most popular places in San Francisco for the past ten years. When you have success like that, the jackals start to circle. There are always people who try to horn in and get a share."

"But . . ."

He shook his head decisively. "I'm not going to listen to any more opposition on this, Hailey. I've found a place for you. It's a resort, really—horses, swimming, peace and quiet. You'll have time to read all those books you keep telling me you've been putting off reading because you just don't have time. You'll be in the nice warm sunshine while the rest of us are still dealing with winter. You'll have the time of your life.''

She knew she was going. Still there were loose ends to tie up. "But my job..." she reminded him. She worked as a buyer for Ganby's Department Store, and she loved the career she was blazing for herself. It would be hard to put it on hold.

She might have known he would already have that problem taken care of. "I've talked to Warren. He understands the situation and he's willing to give you a leave of absence. He'll hold your job for you.''

There had been times when she'd cursed the fact that her boss and her father were good friends, but this seemed to be an instance when it would help rather than hinder. She sighed. They were ganging up on her, weren't they?

"How long will it take?" she asked, her submission already clear in her voice.

He smiled at her. "I don't imagine it will be for longer than three or four weeks at the most.''

"Oh, Daddy.''

He put an arm around her shoulders and drew her closer. "Sugar, I hate to be dictatorial, but you've got to do this. If you don't, I won't be able to testify, and I might have to leave the country.''

She looked at him sideways. He sounded quite sincere and she truly wanted to believe him. He'd lied to her before, lied in ways that had cut into their relationship and almost ruined it. But that was in the past. She'd dealt with it, accepted that he was what he was, and moved on. He was her father. She loved him. And there was absolutely no reason she could think of that he would be hiding anything from her. She decided he had to be telling the truth. This time.

There was nothing left to do but agree. So here she was, and the desert that had once looked magically mysterious now looked hypnotically tedious.

The wind tugged at her scarf as she made the turn onto the ranch roads. Ahead she saw the ranch house, a large, imposing building atop a gentle hill.

"Home sweet home," she murmured to herself sardonically as she pulled up before the entryway. She jumped out of the car and turned to wave as the gray sedan came sliding into the yard. But before the men reached her, she'd opened the boot of her car and pulled out her packages and was starting up the steps into the house.

"With all due respect, you drive too darn fast, Miss Kingston," one of them called to her.

She waved again, laughing, and took the steps two at a time. "Jen?" she called, knowing the house should be empty except for the household staff.

Dressed in the pale blue uniform all the house help wore, Jen came clattering down the stairs, ebony hair flying behind her. "Did you get it?" she cried, her dark eyes sparkling.

"Shh!" Hailey glanced at the back of the hall and put her finger to her lips. "Yes, I got it. Let's go and try it on."

Jen gave her a grin, snatched a couple of her bags from her and whirled. "Great," she said, leading the way back up the stairs. "I can hardly wait to see the transformation."

Hailey followed a bit more slowly. She had struck up something of a friendship with the younger woman who was working as a housekeeper's assistant to pay her way through the nearby college. Together they had hatched a plot to get Hailey out of the house for an evening. The packages she'd picked up in town were the first step. The two of them made their way into the bedroom at the corner of the house and carefully closed the door.

"Here goes nothing," Hailey breathed to herself as she pulled open one of her parcels, a round box, and extracted a dark wig styled in a pixieish cut, holding it up. "Me as an Italian. What do you think?"

"It's darling," Jen cried, fingering the silky hair. "But what are you going to do with all that blond stuff you've got on the top of your head?"

"You'll see," Hailey promised lightly, dropping down before her mirror and deftly pulling strands of her own hair into coils that she expertly pinned to her scalp. Taking the wig in both hands, she carefully tugged it down over the pinned tresses.

"Gosh." Jen shook her head in awe. "Wow, that makes all the difference, doesn't it? I wouldn't have recognized you."

Hailey nodded, looking at her reflection speculatively. "That's the point, isn't it?" she murmured. But it was true. Her thick, gorgeous blond hair had always been her trademark. With the black hair in a pixie cut, she looked like a completely different person. For just a moment, she wondered if it was going to make her act differently, too. "Wild?" she mused to herself. "Daring?"

"It's going to be fun tonight," Jen promised. "You're sure you want to do it?"

"Absolutely." Hailey smiled at her in the mirror, her eyes dancing with anticipation. "If I can get away from my ever-present shadows. They pride themselves on watching every move I make. It is getting really old."

Jen nodded her sympathy. "We'll fool them, don't worry. I got a uniform for you. It's hanging in your closet. It should fit."

"Oh, thanks, Jen." She smiled at the girl. "You're really going to a lot of trouble just to help me get a night out."

Jen smiled back warmly. "It's my pleasure, believe me. Those two cops have been driving us all crazy, ordering us around like we were their servants or something. If we can put this over on Tweedledum and Tweedledummer, it'll be worth every minute."

Hailey laughed. "Okay. Here's the game plan. At dinner, I'm going to whine and howl about the horrible headache I've suddenly come down with. And when I go up to bed, I'm going to warn everyone not to bother me until morning on pain of death."

"Then you'll slip into the wig and uniform and meet me in the kitchen at eight. Okay?"

"Okay."

Jen started for the door, and Hailey called after her.

"Jen . . . thank you again. I really appreciate it."

"No problem," the younger woman said, laughing as she turned and left the room.

"No problem," Hailey echoed, pulling off the wig and looking at herself in the mirror. Of course not. What could go wrong?

Two

With a long afternoon still stretching out before her, Hailey decided to get out her easel and do some sketching. Her pencil drawings were usually quick and small, done on a sketch pad. But this time she was in the mood for something grander, something huge and panoramic, just like this red and gold desert she'd been staring at for three weeks now. So she would need her easel.

It was old-fashioned and heavy, made of wood and hard to carry. She managed to get it into the back of her car by herself, and then, once she'd driven out and found an area she liked, managed to get it out of the car and set it up. But the thought of carrying the heavy easel, as well as all her painting and drawing supplies to the hill where she wanted to set up shop, was daunting.

She looked out toward where her faithful bodyguards had pulled over to keep an eye on her. They seldom got close, but they were always there, and it was darn annoying. She could call them to come help her, she supposed. But she didn't want to do that. That would be similar to admitting she needed them around. And she would never admit that.

She glanced at the car again and saw that they were both getting out. Frowning, she was about to call to them, to protest, but they turned and began to walk toward the high side of the stream. They were moving away, not closer, and she sighed with relief as they melted into the brush and were soon lost from sight. They'd been on sketching expeditions with her before and they obviously expected a long, boring wait, so had hatched a plan with something better to do. She might almost be able to pretend they weren't with her.

Turning back, she examined her surroundings with a practiced eye. The place was the greenest she'd found in the area. The stream running through it nourished a stand of cottonwoods at the base of the hill. The wind was ruffling the leaves, turning the light sides to shimmer in the afternoon sun, when she heard the hoofbeats. A rider was coming.

Leaving her things in a heap, she walked quickly back to the road, ready to hail whoever it might be. It was bound to be a worker on the ranch. Surely he would help her. Shading her eyes with her hand, she watched him approach.

Mitch pulled the horse to a stop easily and looked down at her. Even here in the middle of nowhere, with a bead of sweat rolling down her temple, she looked gorgeous. Her blond hair tumbled about her shoulders and framed her face the way an expensive fur might have. Her green eyes seemed to glitter in the sun, and her perfect skin was slightly flushed.

Everything in him was signaling danger, and he knew the best thing he could do was get out of this situation as quickly as possible. He wasn't sure why she'd flagged him down, but whatever she wanted, he was going to have to avoid it. That meant he would have to be rude. But that didn't really matter. He didn't want to get closer to her, anyway. Being rude might be the best ploy he had going for him.

"Hi, you work here, don't you?" she said with a friendly gesture. "I wonder, could you take a moment to help me, please? I've got some things I want to move, and it's awkward trying to do it on my own, so if you—"

"Sorry, lady," he said coolly, looking toward the horizon. "This is a working ranch. I work the cattle. I'm not trained in guest relations. Get somebody from the house to do it for you."

Her chin went up and her gaze hardened perceptibly. His reaction was unexpected, but she wasn't thrown by it. She'd dealt with recalcitrant personnel before.

For just a moment, she took his measure. His boots were scuffed and worn, and his jeans were snug and almost silver from wear. He certainly looked like a working cowboy. She glanced at his worn, callused hands and his broad shoulders. His face was tanned so dark, his blue eyes seemed startlingly bright. He looked authentic, all right. The only aspect that gave her pause—and she thought she'd noticed it on this man before—was the look in his eyes. There was something too sharp there, something too knowing. Still he claimed to be a cowboy, and a cowboy would suit her fine right now.

"I'm not asking you as an employee, or a house worker, or whatever," she told him, waving a hand in the air. "I'm asking you as a person—one human being to another. Simple request. Nothing complicated."

The determination in her voice was matched by the set of her jaw, and he noted it with something halfway between amusement and annoyance. She was used to ordering people around, wasn't she? Well, that was just too bad. He glanced at his watch, making a show of it and starting to gather the reins together to make his escape. "I'm late. I'm due at the branding shed."

Her eyes blazed. Reaching out, she grabbed hold of the bridle, effectively thwarting his plans to leave immediately. "I could write you a note," she offered tartly. "You could take it to your foreman. Maybe then he would excuse your tardiness."

He looked down at her and she glared back. "Will you please help me?" she asked crisply.

But he was just as stubborn. His jaw could set, too, and his eyes were even colder. "I'm sorry," he said firmly. "I have other things to do."

She gazed at him, not with anger but with speculation. There it was again, that element in him that looked untamed in a way that had nothing to do with sagebrush and desert winds. Something about this cowboy was annoying her, even beyond his refusal to jump down and help her. She realized now she'd seen him before, working around the corral, and even in town that morning. She'd noticed it then, too. There was a measure of contempt in that look he was giving her. Contempt. Now she was even more annoyed. How dare he? People just didn't look at her that way. Especially men.

"Look," she insisted. "I'm not asking you to spend the afternoon with me. I'm merely appealing for help in carrying my easel and supplies up to the top of that hill. I realize this sort of thing is far, far below punching cows, but think of it as charity work, and maybe it will make you feel saintly."

His mouth twitched and his gaze made another arrogant sweep over her. "What makes you think I'm interested in feeling saintly?"

"Oh, I don't know." She waved her hand airily. "Something about you suggests you might be able to use a few brownie points in heaven. I'll bet you don't rack up too many of them during your normal day, do you?"

For all his antipathy toward getting involved, he had to admit she was waging a pretty good fight here. "I try to avoid them," he said dryly, but he didn't pull away and urge the horse back onto the road as he should have. In fact, he was forgetting about his desire to move on for the moment.

"Obviously," she taunted good-naturedly. "But this time, you see, you're trapped."

His head went back and he let out a short laugh. "The hell I am."

She shrugged grandly. "Well, that's right where I'm afraid you're headed if you don't get a few good works un-

der your belt. So you see, I'm trying to do *you* a favor." She
gestured with a toss of her head, all supreme confidence.
"Come on down and help."

He met her eyes and stared for a long moment. He wasn't
about to change his overall opinion of her, but he had to
admit there was more in her than he'd been giving her credit
for. And he also knew they had come to a point where it
would be churlish of him to continue refusing to help her.
How had he let this happen? He was usually the one ma-
nipulating things. This time, she was going to win. Smiling
ruefully to himself, he swung down off the horse.

"What do you want carried?" he asked her without ran-
cor.

She breathed a sigh of relief. She hadn't been about to let
him know how shaky her confidence had become in the past
few minutes. Looking at him now, so tall, so thickly muscular, wearing faded jeans and a plaid shirt augmented by a
leather vest, she knew he was all male and decidedly insolent. And here she was, ordering him around.

And here he was, giving in. My my. She allowed herself a
quick feeling of satisfaction.

"This easel," she told him, gesturing toward it. "I can
actually carry the rest myself."

He nodded, glancing at her face. To her credit, she didn't
gloat, but took his acquiescence as a matter of course and
went on with things. "That won't be a problem," he said.

She was still weighing possibilities, her hands on her hips,
her head to the side. "Maybe you could just prop it up on
your horse." She frowned at the large beast doubtfully.

Mitch patted his neck. "This big fella is skittish as it is. If
I start piling wood on him, he's liable to take it as a very bad
sign."

She nodded thoughtfully. "You're probably right. Well,
if you just took one side and I took the other..."

Without waiting for the rest of her musing, he lifted the
easel without effort and hoisted it onto his wide shoulder.
"Top of that hill?" he asked, nodding toward the area.

"Yes," she said, hastily gathering her other things. "Thank you so much."

But he was already striding toward the spot and she had to run to catch up by the time he reached it. He set the easel in place and was going to take her bundle of papers from her, but as she transferred the items, a small stack of drawings fell out and sailed haphazardly to the ground. Picking one of them up, he stopped, startled, staring at the cowboy face she'd drawn. Slowly he turned and stared at her, feeling like a man walking on quicksand.

"What the hell are you doing here?" he asked her softly, waving the picture at her. "That's me."

She glanced at it, not surprised at all. "Oh. Is it? Yes, I guess it is. I was just sketching some of the cowboys a week or so ago. I didn't remember that you were one of them."

He stared at her with steely eyes for a long moment, then handed the sketch back to her. "Don't do it again," he warned, his voice low but ominous.

She looked up at him, somewhat startled by his tone. "Why not?"

Yes, why not? He could hardly explain that he was an undercover agent, could he? That he didn't want his cover blown. "It's an invasion of privacy," he said, evading the real issue. That made her laugh.

"Oh, come on. I was just sketching character studies. As far as I was concerned, you were just an ordinary cowboy, no more, no less. It was nothing personal."

He didn't relent, and actually, he had to admit, seeing the picture of himself had been downright disconcerting. It gave him an eerie feeling, as though something were going on here that he didn't understand. And he hated not feeling in the know.

"Still," he said, looking at her narrowly, "you reached out and took a piece of me and I didn't even know it. Some Indian tribes used to think you captured someone's soul when you had a picture of them."

She waved that theory away dismissively. "That was photography."

He shrugged. "Same difference." His forefinger jabbed at the picture. "That's me, and anyone looking at it is going to know it's me."

And that was just the problem. She was damn good, but he wasn't about to tell her so. Opening the sketchbook he was holding, he riffled through others that were just as well-done.

"You see," she said, watching him, "they're just character studies. I mean, I don't think of you as you, whoever that may be. I think of you as Joe Cowboy."

He nodded, studying her work. "Sort of a generic brand," he said softly.

"Exactly."

Looking up, he pinned her with a sharp gaze as he snapped the book shut. "Sure, I understand that," he said calmly. "That's kind of the way I think of you."

That startled her. She turned slowly, keeping her face bland. "Oh, really?"

"Sure." His eyes narrowed. "You're the generic rich girl."

Her eyes widened and she laughed. "Hardly."

Straightening, he handed her back her sketchbook. "Didn't your father buy out the place so you could have it to yourself for a month?"

She opened her mouth to protest, but after all, what could she say? He was pretty near the mark. "You don't know the first thing about it," she said simply.

He shrugged, his hard face unemotional. "All I know is, they booted all the other guests out so you wouldn't be disturbed. And you have two bodyguards. Now what kind of message do you think all that is sending?"

She stared at him for a moment, then turned and began to straighten the easel, preparing it for work. "My father used to say, if you want to send a message, call the telegraph people," she murmured as she aligned the paper guides.

He knew he deserved that, and he almost smiled. "I'll keep that in mind," he told her instead. "Now, if you've finished with me, boss-lady, I'll get back to work."

She turned her green gaze on him and shook her head in wonder. "You've got your nerve, mister," she said. "It's pretty obvious you've never been briefed in customer relations." She tilted her head to the side, studying him. "Aren't you afraid I'll turn you in? That you might lose your job?"

He shifted his weight from one leg to the other, ready to make his escape. "Miss Kingston," he drawled, "there are things in this life I am afraid of. Losing this crummy job isn't one of them." He started to turn away, but said back over his shoulder, "And neither are you."

"Then what are you afraid of?" she called after him. "I'd be interested in knowing."

He paused, still looking back. "I'm more afraid of losing my self-respect than I am of losing this job," he told her seriously.

She laughed softly. "What is your name, cowboy?"

He hesitated. "Mitch Harper," he said at last, rather grudgingly. "Happy sketching, Miss Kingston."

She smiled. "Happy branding, Mitch Harper. Be kind to those little dogies."

For a moment he stood there looking at her, like an animal poised just before flight. The picture she made with her wild blond hair and the blue sky behind her made him want to stand and stare for a long, long time. But he controlled the impulse and moved on. That was what cowboys always did, wasn't it? They moved on, moseyed on out of there. But he knew this little encounter had changed things. She wouldn't ignore him the next time they met. The dynamics had changed. For some inexplicable reason, he began to whistle as he made his way back to where his horse was tied.

Hailey watched him go and shook her head. Then she turned to her easel and began to sketch rapidly, first the rough outline of a man, then the details, and before Mitch had disappeared from sight, she had a new picture of him. Standing back to examine it, she smiled. Then she tore off the sheet and quickly began drawing him from another angle, forgetting all about the landscape work she'd planned to do. Was she interested in his form because of something in him that had inspired her? Or was she merely happy to do something he'd expressly ordered her not to attempt? She wasn't sure. Maybe a little of both. Whatever motivated her, she worked for hours, and when she was done, she had ten pictures of the man, and it made her smile to think of presenting them all to him, neatly tied in a satin bow.

"Later," she promised herself as she packed up her charcoals and pencils. Right now, she had to begin preparing for the dance she was going to attend tonight.

Tonight. Ah, tonight. Maybe a little romance. Maybe... maybe just one.

Folding the easel and putting it under a bush for future use, she walked happily back through the grass. All in all, this had been one of the least boring days since she'd arrived, and with the evening ahead of her, it promised to keep right on going that way.

Mitch left the confines of the bunkhouse and wandered out under the stars. He could hear the raucous poker game going on behind him. Ordinarily he liked to join in. But tonight he was restless. Instead of heading toward the edge of the driveway, where he could look out over the valley in the moonlight, he turned toward the house. The place was lit up as though it were full of guests, as it usually was at this time of year. But there was only Hailey Kingston. Hailey and her bodyguards and a house full of help. It seemed like a waste.

He knew only sketchy details of the case. Her father was involved in a trial in San Francisco. As he understood it, the man had gangland ties that the district attorney's office had been suspicious of for some time, and now he was paying for his misdeeds. Just what they were, Mitch wasn't sure.

"He probably didn't pay his taxes," he muttered to himself as he sauntered along. That was the one crime the government could never forgive or overlook. At any rate, there was a lot of missing money involved, as well as some documents. The D.A. thought Hailey might have an idea where those things were hidden. And Mitch was here to see if she would inadvertently give a clue as to where they might be.

He'd had cases like this before, but they weren't his favorite. He preferred going after the bad guys directly, not through some woman. Unless the woman herself was a bad guy, of course. Now those cases could be a lot of fun.

But this case wasn't exactly topping the charts in the fun department. It was assignments like these that made him wonder why he'd ever gotten into this business, why he didn't get out and go start up his own business somewhere.

But he wasn't going to change, and he knew why. He hadn't needed therapy to get to the bottom of his own motivations. It was clear as a bell to him. He knew it had to do with his background, with his father's failures and his own experience of being raised as a rescuer, always pulling his family back from the brink of disaster. He just couldn't stand to see the bad guys win. He had to make sure they met their just deserts. That was also the impetus that made him side with the underdog every time. Growing up, he'd been down so far, normal life looked like a climb up a heavenly stairway to him. He wanted to make sure that didn't happen to good people if he could help it.

He glanced up at Hailey's bedroom window as he neared the house. The light was on, but as he watched, the window went dark. She was already going to bed, it seemed. He'd heard from one of the dinner servers he'd struck up a casual relationship with that she'd gone to her room early with a bad headache. So that, it appeared, was that, at least for this evening.

He smiled when he thought about their encounter that afternoon. He had to admit, she had spirit. And the funny thing was, he had a feeling she was just as bored with this extended vacation in the country as he was.

"So do us both a favor and go home already," he advised the darkened window. But he didn't think she would take his advice.

Standing hidden in the shadow of the trees, he watched as Jen came out of the house by the back door and turned to call to someone else. Another of the staff joined her, a woman he hadn't noticed before. She was pretty, with a fluid walk that turned his head. He whistled below his breath. How had he overlooked this one? That was something he was going to have to rectify.

But right now, he had other things on his mind and he hardly paid attention as the two women got into a small economy car and began to maneuver out of the tricky parking place. He could see through a side window that the two cops were playing cards in the game room. This might be an opportunity to gather more information. He looked back toward the parking area and saw that Jen and her fellow worker were driving off down the road. Starting toward the house, he mused over whether he would question the butler or strike up a conversation with the boy who did the dishes.

For just a moment, he thought about the night he'd climbed the brick chimney to gain access to Hailey's bedroom while she was down eating dinner. He wasn't supposed to do things like that—not officially, at any rate. But you could find out things by looking through the possessions of people under surveillance that you couldn't find out any other way, and he'd been getting antsy. What he'd seen had surprised him. She had lots of quality clothing, but nothing fancy, no fur coats, no diamonds. Expensive things, the sort that were made to last, but not to be showy. Good, basic clothing. If he hadn't known better, he would have thought she was a woman of uncommon class. And she certainly had the body to wear anything and make it look good. But it was also obvious she came from money.

"Of course," he whispered to himself. "Otherwise, I wouldn't be watching her, now would I?"

He'd almost reached the back porch when something visceral struck him and he spun, staring at the cloud of dust behind Jen's car as her taillights disappeared around the bend. The picture Jen's companion had made replayed itself in his brain. Short, dark hair, a staff uniform...

"And the longest damn legs this side of the Great Divide," he muttered savagely. It had been Hailey Kingston, hadn't it? Hailey in disguise and running away from her bodyguards. What was the matter with him? How could he have missed such an obvious ploy?

"Damn it," he snarled to himself, starting toward his truck at a run. "Get your mind straight and do your job!"

The dust had settled by the time he reached the main road and he had to make a choice. Right or left? He thought he remembered that Jen lived in the foothills, so he turned toward them and was rewarded in a few moments by the sight of her taillights ahead. Slowing, he followed until they turned into a small community and pulled up in front of an apartment building. Driving on past, he parked half a block away and waited, engine and lights turned off. His instincts told him it would only be a few moments before they would be out again, and once more he was right. They'd shed their uniforms and were dressed in bright skirts and big sleeves.

"What are they doing, going square dancing?" he asked himself as he eased his car out behind theirs again.

Sure enough, Jen drove up in front of a long, low building about two miles from her apartment. Mustang Café, the sign said. Music poured out the door. Mitch watched as Jen and the woman he was now sure was Hailey got out of the car and hurried toward the entrance. Heaving a sigh, he tilted his head back and asked himself just how much square dancing music he could stand. Not much. And there didn't really seem much point to it, anyway. He might as well head for home. She wasn't going to be doing anything relevant here.

He'd already pulled the car onto the highway when he saw a familiar face in a car going the other way. It took a minute to register the identity of the man, but as he watched him turn into the dance club, it came back to him. Pauly McVern. That was who it was. He ran a small private detective agency out of Palm Springs, catering mostly to strip club

owners and gambling interests. What the hell was he doing
here?

So much for a quick ride home. Mitch heaved another
sigh as he turned the truck and headed back for the parking
lot. If Pauly was sniffing around, he'd better go in and see
if he could figure out what was up. There was just no way
to avoid it.

"Hee-haw and howdy," he muttered. "Here we come."

Three

Hailey stepped inside the Western dance club and looked from one side to the other. Energy washed over her in a wave that was almost physical—the noise, the laughter, the music, the smoke, the color of the lights, the heat from a lot of people in a very small space. For just a moment, she hesitated in the doorway. She'd been bored, she'd been climbing the walls, and she'd wanted so badly to get away from those two bumpkin bodyguards and go out and do something. But was this really what she'd had in mind?

Not exactly. But what did she want, anyway? What had she come here for? This was a dance club where people got together to have fun, or to pick up a quick date, or to find the man of her dreams. She wasn't expecting the last two. All she'd bargained for was the first. Fun. That was it. So here she was in a silly black wig, looking for fun.

"Come on," Jen was saying impatiently, gesturing for her to come along into the lively room. "I'll show you around this place. It's so neat."

Neat, was it? Hailey hid a smile as she followed her friend. The difference in their ages was a stark reality at times. Jen's eyes were wide with the excitement of being here, and Hailey was wondering why she'd come. She'd been to places like this before—maybe too often.

"The bar is around that way," Jen said, pointing out a long area where cocktail waitresses in tiny cowgirl outfits held trays high above the crowd. "The restaurant is in through that doorway, and then, out here in back..." She led Hailey through an opening into a courtyard where an arbor of tangled red roses circled a wishing well. "Lovers' walk," she said, gazing with wistful admiration at the romantic setting, lights muted, roses blooming around a shimmering wishing well. "Isn't it adorable?"

"I suppose so," Hailey said doubtfully. "If you go in for that sort of thing."

"Oh, you." Jen scoffed at her playfully. "You put on this big old front, but if the right guy came along, you'd give him a tumble, just like any of us. Wouldn't you?"

Hailey smiled at her. She wanted to say no, because that was what the answer was, but she hated to be so cynical when Jen was so full of joyful wonder. "Sure," she said instead. "You're probably right."

"Of course I am." It was evident Jen couldn't conceive of a woman who didn't need a man in her life. "Well, I doubt if you're going to find your kind of male in this place. It's full of cowboys and guys like that. But you can have some fun."

Hailey nodded brightly. "That's what I came for."

"Good." Her face grew more serious. "Just remember, if we see anyone from the ranch, we have to leave right away. Okay? We can't risk them recognizing us."

Hailey frowned. They hadn't really explored the possibility of being found out before. "Jen, what would happen if we get caught? To you, I mean."

The younger woman shrugged. "I'd probably get fired." Reaching out, she grabbed Hailey's hand as she saw the horrified expression spreading across her face. "Oh, don't

worry. Please don't. Don't even think about it. We're here
to have fun.''

Hailey had questioned her own judgment in coming here
from the beginning, and now she was absolutely disgusted
with herself. Why hadn't she thought this thing through and
realized the jeopardy she was putting Jen in? "You're the
generic rich girl," her unhelpful cowboy had accused her
that very afternoon, and she'd denied it. But here she was,
acting as though that were exactly the case.

"Jen, let's get out of here right now," she said earnestly.
"I hadn't realized—"

"Are you kidding?" Jen pulled back and turned toward
the music. "Not on your life. I'm going to dance! Come
on."

Hailey shook her head ruefully. "You go ahead," she
said. "I'll be along in a few minutes."

"Okay," Jen responded happily. "But if I get lucky right
away, you'll find me on the dance floor."

"Okay." She watched Jen hurry toward the crowd and
sighed. Well, here she was, having fun. Funny. It didn't feel
very different from being bored.

"You're just a spoiled rich girl," she chided herself,
thinking of the cowboy again. "Never satisfied." And for
just a moment, she had to wonder if the man wasn't right.

Mitch pulled the truck into a parking place and got out.
Pauly was already out of sight. Striding quickly, he found
his way inside the roadhouse. The room was a kaleidoscope
of lights and sound. The music provided the beat, the
dancers provided the swirling skirts and stomping boots.
The place was packed and everyone seemed to be having a
real good time.

Pushing his Stetson down as low as he could without
blocking off vision altogether, he scanned the room for
Pauly and found him lingering in the fringes, glancing at
something in his hand.

That was all the information Mitch needed to make a
quick diagnosis of the situation. Pauly was very possibly

looking for Hailey. And the last thing Mitch wanted was for the sleazy detective to find her.

At least he was using a photograph for identification. That meant he'd never seen her face-to-face. It also meant he might not recognize her in the disguise. But he didn't like to count on luck.

Moving quickly, he searched through the crowd, glancing at each feminine face. Where the heck was she? And, for that matter, what was he going to do when he found her? Bundle her up and carry her back to the ranch?

Hardly that. He didn't want to come face-to-face with her, in fact. If he did, it would blow his cover. No, he had to think of some way to keep her out of Pauly's clutches without revealing himself. This was going to be tricky.

He scanned the length of the bar, but she wasn't there. Looking back, he saw Pauly coming in behind him, and he melted into the crowd. He'd never spoken to the man and he didn't think he would be recognized, but he couldn't be too careful.

Making his way among the dancers, he gazed at each face but didn't find what he was looking for. He saw Jen, but Hailey wasn't with her. Where had she gone? The rest room was a possibility, but he couldn't follow her in there. Still he could get close.

He turned down the hall to the telephones, and suddenly there she was, coming toward him. Adrenaline pumped as he turned, looking for an escape, but a crowd of laughing women had come into the hallway behind him and were about to carry him along in their wave of raucous celebration. He glanced back down the hall. Hailey was headed straight at him. No time to duck out. Her eyes met his and widened.

Yes, he thought to himself, resignedly. *We have recognition.* Now what? She'd seen him. They were going to have to speak. He was going to have to think fast, find a cover story, something....

Working on pure instinct, he stopped, looked down at her and smiled as the laughing women swarmed around them and moved on. Meanwhile, he was thinking to himself, *Here goes nothing—playboy act number one, sticking to basics.*

"Hi," he said aloud, letting his eyes do his flirting for him, as though she were the cutest thing he'd ever seen, and what's more, someone he'd never seen before. This had to have all the earmarks of a spontaneous pick up. And it had to be very convincing. He tilted his chin and gave her a rakish look from beneath the brim of his hat. "Where've you been all my life?"

Her mouth dropped open and she merely stared. She'd seen him too late to make her own getaway, and her heart had fallen. Her first thought was that she'd been caught, and not only was she going to be in big trouble, so was Jen. But now he was acting as though he didn't realize who she was. Could it be? No. She couldn't be that lucky. "Uh..." She could manage no more on such short notice.

"You from around here?" he asked, still in flirt mode, his blue eyes holding her gaze. "Because if you are, and we haven't met before, something is definitely wrong with the system."

Her pretty brows drew together and she searched his eyes. Was it possible that he really didn't recognize her? And if so, how could she make sure she didn't do anything to set him off?

"Uh..." she murmured again, afraid to speak for fear of giving herself away. She blinked at him, feeling like a half-wit, and then looked down at where her fingers were twisting together painfully. He knew who she was, surely. How could he not? They'd just been talking together that afternoon. Though as she remembered it, he hadn't smiled at her once. Now he was all smiles. She swallowed hard. He was waiting for an answer.

"I...I'm just visiting," she said softly, then stared at his eyes, waiting for awareness to light a spark there.

But it didn't seem to happen.

"That's a shame," he said with a wicked grin. "Then we'll have to work fast. We have so little time to get to know each other."

Now she was amused. He really didn't know who she was. He was giving her what she could only assume was his standard come-on line of bull. And that was interesting—the cowboy she'd met this afternoon hadn't been interested in striking up a relationship. The wig made all the difference, it seemed. Her hand rose involuntarily and she touched it lightly. It made her look different. It made her act differently. Why wouldn't it make her talk differently? Yes.

She took a deep breath, wondering if she could really pull this off. Determinedly she squared her shoulders and thought country.

"I'm afraid you're wrong there," she told him pertly, managing to change her voice into something that seemed to fit the mood of the place. She made it a little higher and put on a bit of a country drawl. That was the key. She would put on an accent. "We don't have any time at all. Sorry, mister, but I don't know you from Adam."

She waited, breathless, to see how he would react to that, but he merely grinned again.

"Of course not," he said smoothly, though he thought, *Whoa, the old voice trick,* as he looked down at her. "You're just visiting. Remember?" he said aloud. "How could you know me?" His gaze took on a significant slant. "But we're going to have to remedy that situation right away."

She blinked up at him and took another deep breath. It was okay. Even the voice hadn't tipped him off. She just might get away with this after all. Looking past him, she began to edge away.

"No thanks," she said crisply. "I'm afraid I'm busy."

He shifted his weight just enough to block her escape route. Glancing back into the dance club, he didn't catch sight of Pauly, but he knew the detective had to be out there somewhere. It was very likely Pauly would be fooled by the wig, but he didn't want to take chances. Much as he hated to admit it, he was going to have to stick with her for a while. And that meant he was going to have to take her out on the dance floor. Not his favorite thing to do, but he didn't have much choice. He looked back down at her with a shadowed gaze.

"Let's put it this way. Would you like to dance?"

She gazed up at him blankly. "Dance?" she echoed. Dance with the cowboy who'd treated her with sarcasm and scorn just hours before? He had to be joking.

He shrugged and gestured toward the large open room behind him. "Isn't that what you came for?"

She had to admit, he had her there. "I can't," she said, unable to come up with a good excuse on the spur of the moment, though what she wanted most of all was to find a way to lose this man and not see him again tonight. "I mean, I really shouldn't...."

Mitch's habit was to cut to the chase. "Do you have a date waiting for you?" he asked, not sure at that point what her answer would be. For all he knew, this entire escapade was set up for her to meet someone. For all he knew, she'd done it before.

She hesitated, biting her lip. "What if I do?" she asked.

He shrugged and let a warm, comical look fill his eyes. "Then point him out and I'll ask his permission."

Despite everything, she had to laugh. "My, aren't you old-fashioned."

It was his turn to drawl. "It's just the old cowboy code." He tipped his hat with his forefinger to the brim. "We all have our standards."

"Right. Like honor among thieves."

He gave her a pained look. "Such cynicism from such a pretty lady. And all I did was ask her to dance."

She was losing ground and she knew it. It didn't look as if she were going to be able to get away without a turn around the dance floor. The thought of it made her heart beat a little faster. It would be dangerous to be so close for so long. Suppose he noticed something? Suppose the truth finally dawned on him? But at the same time, to keep turning him down would be odd in itself. After all, he was right. She'd come to dance. Why not with him? She was going to have to bite the bullet.

"Well, all right," she said grudgingly, remembering to give her voice a country twang. "Just one dance."

He turned and gestured with a flourish for her to precede him. As they entered the larger room, he managed to look casual as he quickly surveyed the landscape. He caught a glimpse of Pauly heading for the back of the building where a space had been set aside for pool tables and video games and he breathed a sigh of relief. Pauly was going to check out the area and then maybe he would give up and leave.

Well, that did change things. Maybe he could get out of this dancing stuff after all. He'd never been much for dancing, and now that he was facing the music, he began to search about for an excuse to avoid it.

"You know, it's kind of hot in here," he began as a new idea occurred to him. Maybe he could get her to go out and walk in the courtyard with him instead of dancing. "I thought maybe..."

But he was too late. Now that they were out in the main room, the lively music was infecting her with the mood of the moment.

"The music is starting," she said, lifting her chin. "Let's go." She hooked her arm through his and smiled at him, anticipation dancing in her green eyes.

He was stuck. Looking around at the dancers, he began to realize there was no way he was going to get away with slow-dancing here. "I don't know. I'm not sure I know this dance."

"Oh, it's just line dancing." She tugged on his arm. "Anybody can do it. Here. I'll show you."

The next thing he knew, he was two-stepping across the floor, his thumbs hooked into his wide belt, and she was laughing up into his face. It felt awkward at first. He wasn't much of a dancer. But she was right—it was easy. And she looked good in her flouncy skirt, whirling in front of him. In a few moments, he was having almost as much fun as she seemed to be having.

The tempo changed and she slid into his arms as naturally as though they were old friends.

"'Cowboys Never Fall in Love,'" she murmured, naming the song that was playing. "Do you believe that?"

He grinned. "I live it," he said lightly.

She laughed, but at that moment he saw Pauly come back into the room and he pulled Hailey closer to him. She swayed with him, her head nestling into the hollow of his shoulder, while he maneuvered her around so that she was always with her back to the detective. But Pauly kept moving, and it was hard to keep up.

"What are you so nervous about?" Hailey asked suddenly, pulling her head back so she could look into his face.

"Me? I'm not nervous." He gave her a smile that was all innocence.

"You keep looking over your shoulder." She frowned, peering past him. "Have you got somebody following you?"

If he'd been a little less experienced, he might have blushed. Her guess was just too close to the mark for comfort.

"Why do you say that?" he asked instead.

She searched his gaze, then shrugged. "Oh, I don't know. I thought maybe your ex-wife was having you tailed or something."

He gazed at her quizzically. "What gives you the idea that I have an ex-wife?"

Her green eyes clouded. Did he really need an explanation? He was a man. He must know what men were like.

"A lot of men like you have ex-wives lurking in the shadows," she said, trying for a flippant tone, "or hiding in a closet somewhere, ready to leap out and yell boo when you least expect it."

"I see." He frowned, not liking the sound of that. What had happened to this woman? It was pretty obvious there was pain behind those beautiful eyes. Funny. It was hard to picture anyone this attractive with a broken heart. But broken hearts did come in all shapes and sizes.

"You sound like someone who's had a bit of experience with this leaping and yelling stuff," he said softly. It was not part of his nature to inquire into things like this, but he wanted to find out more about her, what made her tick—at least that was what he told himself.

She managed a small smile. "The leaping and yelling may be a bit of an exaggeration," she admitted. No, there hadn't been much leaping and yelling, but there had been enough lying and hiding of true feelings to last her a lifetime. Why was it that men seemed to think beautiful women were trophies, that they didn't have any value other than as prizes to be won and bragged about? She'd had her share of heartache over that sort of thing when she was very young and it had taught her life's lessons early. You couldn't believe what a man said, especially when he said he loved you. The word *love* was a tool he used to get what he wanted. The word *no* was a tool she used to make sure he didn't reach his goal.

"Anyway, I don't worry about things like that any longer," she said airily. "I leave that to others."

"But not you."

"No, not me." Her eyes were guileless. "I'm very careful."

He cocked one dark eyebrow. "How's that?"

"I don't date unless I am absolutely certain..." She paused and bit her lip, wondering how to explain it in terms he might understand.

"Until you're absolutely certain he's crazy about you?" he asked idly.

She looked at him, amused at how far off the mark he was. "No. Until I'm absolutely certain there is no romantic feeling between us. I only date men who don't fall for me. It's the only way to be sure."

He shook his head, not sure he'd heard right. "Wait a minute. That's crazy," he said.

The music had stopped and they were standing at the edge of the crowd, still together but not touching, not doing anything that might commit them as a couple. They were both being very careful of that.

"That really doesn't make any sense," he stated flatly, ready to go on.

But before he had a chance to launch into his reasons for bewilderment, a handsome, clean-cut young man broke from a nearby group and smiled at Hailey. "Are you... would you like to dance?" he asked her shyly before he noticed Mitch.

Hailey smiled at the young man and began to shake her head. At the same time, as he glanced over her black wig, Mitch could see Pauly disappearing out the front door of the establishment. Pauly was gone, and the reason for dogging her every move left with him. He looked down at her. It had been fun, but it was over now.

"She'd love to," he told the startled youth. Giving Hailey a wink, he began to turn away. "Listen, you came to dance and to have some fun. I guess I ought to let you do that."

"Oh, but—" She put out a hand, as though she were about to reach for him, and then drew it back quickly. His abrupt change of plan was startling. Men rarely turned and ran from her. She was going to need a moment or two to adjust to shifting sands.

"Here you go." He practically handed her off to the other man, but before he left, he gave her a bittersweet smile. "Treat her gently," he told the young man. "She's a special lady."

Hailey watched him turn on his heel and melt into the crowd. A part of her resented him saying that. And another part was glowing in response. What on earth had made him leave her so suddenly? Had he recognized her? But no, if he'd recognized her, he would have said something. He was a strange man. But she couldn't say she was sorry they'd met tonight.

Still, this was ridiculous. She didn't act like this. She didn't ever let a man get to her. And she wasn't about to start now.

"Excuse me. Miss?"

"Oh." Turning, she smiled at the young man she'd forgotten about. "Sorry. Let's dance, shall we?" Taking his hand, she joined him as the fiddles began a wild country song.

She did a lot of dancing after that. She danced to slow tunes, she danced to fast tunes, and she spent most of the time hopping around to protect her feet. She danced with a college boy who'd had too much to drink and a truck driver who told dirty jokes and a cop who talked in a very gruff voice and a large, very handsome man who held her too close and wanted to take her out to see the moon, and a short, funny man who tried to trick her into revealing her telephone number. And every once in a while, she caught sight of Mitch standing along the edge of the crowd, watching her.

That was strange. Why didn't he dance? Was he trying to figure out who she was and where he'd seen her before? No, she didn't think that was it.

That wasn't the look she saw in his eyes. Just what that look was, she couldn't quite pin down. But she knew it wasn't puzzled inquiry. No, that wasn't it.

He was certainly a different man here than the cowboy she'd had the run-in with that afternoon. She'd felt she knew him, after their confrontation and then all the sketching she'd done of him. She knew his face, knew his long, muscular body, but she obviously didn't know him at all. And as he watched her but refused to come close, her curiosity grew.

Now and then she ran into Jen and they exchanged greetings, but every time her friend was in the arms of the same blond cowboy, and from the smitten look on her face, Hailey figured Jen thought she'd found what she'd come for.

It was getting late, and her feet were getting tired. The wig was itchy and she was ready to go home. The dancing had been fun, but she'd had enough now, and she slipped away from the crowd and looked around the room for Mitch.

He'd disappeared. She wandered the edges of the group, then looked in the pool table room and the card room, but she didn't see him. Disappointed, she made one last try and peeked into the bar area. There he was at the end of the counter, nursing a shot glass full of something dark and evil looking. Her spirits brightened immediately, and she headed straight for him.

Mitch was having his first and last drink of the night, and he wasn't sure why he'd felt he needed it. But when he saw her coming across the room, he was glad he'd fortified himself. Something told him she wasn't just going to say goodbye and head out the door. Chances were, he was in for another session with this bewildering woman.

He didn't know what he was still doing here. He should have left long ago. At first he'd told himself he was watching Hailey in case Pauly came back. But as time went by, that had worn thin, and he'd had to admit it was more than that. He had to watch her because he couldn't stop watching her. Not a good sign.

But he was surprised that she'd searched him out this way. After all, it had been obvious from the beginning that she was very anxious that he not realize who she was. The more contact they had, the more chance that he would put two and two together. Still she'd come looking for him. He wondered why that was.

"Hi," she said, plopping down on the bar stool beside his. "Wow, I'm about danced out."

He gave her a long, slow stare. He was getting used to the short, cropped look. She would be beautiful shaved bald, but he hoped he'd never have to see it. "Hey, pretty lady," he said softly. "May I buy you a drink?"

"I'd love one," she responded without hesitation. "I would be forever in your debt."

An intriguing prospect. He raised an eyebrow. "What would you like?" he asked her.

"A tall, frosty glass of iced tea," she said promptly. "That would hit the spot."

He made a gesture to the bartender and in no time, she had exactly what she'd ordered. Taking a long sip, she sighed happily and sat back, looking at him. It was the first time she'd seen him without the hat. His hair was thick and black and curling around the edges, badly in need of a cut.

She liked the way it framed his face. In fact, to her surprise, she liked a lot of things about him.

He watched her curiously, wondering what she was thinking. After all, she knew exactly who he was. Or, at least, she knew him as an employee at the ranch. But she could pretend she didn't know that, just like he was pretending not to realize she was Hailey Kingston. There was a strange sort of logic at work here, but he wasn't sure if it could hold up much longer.

She stretched, her eyes half-closed, and let her head fall back. "I'll never dance again," she promised herself.

He held back a smile. "You seemed to be having a pretty good time when I was watching you."

"Did I?" She made a movement that usually would have resulted in tossing back her thick blond hair, but since that was pinned tightly to her head and covered by the black wig, it didn't work this time and she stopped it in mid-move, feeling awkward.

"Especially when you were dancing with that tall fellow with the beard," Mitch said dryly. "He seemed to spend a lot of time whispering sweet nothings in your ear."

She laughed and the sound was as natural and unselfconscious as water in a brook. "Those weren't sweet nothings at all. He was trying to get me to join the Land and Forest Party. Something about how much fun we would have dashing about in the woods with bushes on our heads." She grinned. "I told him I would have to go home and get permission from my houseplants before I could make a commitment like that."

"Good move." The corners of his mouth twitched and he regarded her speculatively, cupping his shot glass, nursing the drink rather than imbibing. He liked the way she moved, the way she laughed. She was open and spontaneous, like a gawky teenager who'd grown up into an elegant beauty but still retained the natural joy of her younger self. Was it all an act? He was beginning to doubt it.

"But tell me something," he said slowly, remembering what she'd said, when they were dancing, about not dating men who fell for her. "If you're not looking for that 'special' man, and you don't really enjoy the dancing and the meeting of strangers, why are you here?"

She met his gaze and searched it for a moment. He still didn't seem to recognize her. Strange. He seemed too bright to be fooled this way. Could it possibly be that he didn't want to know? That he was enjoying this pretense as much as she was? Because, after all, back at the ranch, they weren't supposed to have anything to do with each other. And here, all contrasts were gone.

"Let's not talk about me," she said, taking another sip of tea. "Let's talk about you." She smiled at him. "So tell me about you. All about you. Where you're from and where you're going."

That was the last thing he could tell her about. "I'll tell you this," he said, instead of launching into an autobiographical sketch. "I'm still sitting here wondering why you won't date men who like you."

"Oh. Well, never mind that." She frowned, annoyed with herself for having brought it up, and waved the entire concept away with a motion of her hand. "I shouldn't have even gotten into that."

"But you did," he said, still toying negligently with his drink.

She did a double take, intrigued by the sound of something she couldn't identify in his voice, something between humor and regret. "I guess I did," she admitted. "But that shouldn't affect you."

He shook his head ruefully. "No, you see, it's more than that." His smile was knowingly bashful, like a grown man playing at being a child. "I'm afraid it's going to disqualify me."

Her mouth formed a perfect "O" for a moment and then she laughed softly. "Why?" she said, looking him straight in the eye. "Do you like me?"

He smiled back, his blue eyes hooded. "I'm considering it."

She stared at him for a moment, all humor draining from her eyes. Reaching out, she circled his wrist with her fingers. "Don't," she urged, only half kidding. "It doesn't pay. Believe me, Platonic is my middle name."

He stared down at where her fingers were touching him. "Friends forever, lovers never?" he asked softly.

"That's it." She took her hand away and wrapped it around her frosty glass. "And please don't tell me how you've got a way about you so special, it'll change my mind. I'm tired of hearing that."

She had been hurt. Someone somewhere had hurt her badly, whether she would admit it or not. And he was a damn fool for letting it get to him. He was coming too close here. He had to climb back down from the edge of the cliff.

This was a very dangerous situation he'd gotten himself into. He didn't want to get close. He couldn't. He had a job to do. But besides that, he never did get close to women. He'd had lovers, even dated steadily for months at a time. But he never let a woman get to him, get in where he really lived. He wasn't made for relationships. He was made to go out into the world and get the bad guys, and that was what he did. He'd never known a woman yet who had tempted him to look for anything else in life. And he didn't think he ever would. If she was intent upon keeping a distance, that was okay with him. In fact, it made him like her better. Platonic, was it? Great. He let her words sink in for a moment, then shook his head.

"Don't worry," he said, staring down into his drink again. "I never beg."

But she knew that already. Just looking at his hard face told her that. "Is that why you backed off so fast out there on the dance floor?" she asked him, partly as a way to change the subject. "I couldn't quite figure it out. One minute you're the playboy of the Western World, and the next, you're handing me over like yesterday's yogurt."

"Yesterday's yogurt?" he repeated, lip curling.

"Well, it's the only thing I could think of on short notice," she replied airily. "But the point is, you couldn't get away fast enough. How come?"

He couldn't very well tell her the truth, but he couldn't think of anything much better, either, so he made do with flippancy and a seductive grin. "Maybe I'd had my five minutes of heaven and it was time to go. I'd used up my allotment."

She made a face at him. "Oh gosh, now you're talking like the playboy again. I don't know. Which one is the real you?"

"The real me." He pondered that for a moment, cupping his drink in his hands. "Now that's a hard one. I don't think I'm up to getting into that tonight. I might have to dig down too many layers to find out."

She frowned, looking at him. "Okay. But you don't mind if I try to connect some of the dots, do you? For instance, what do you do?"

"For a living?"

She nodded.

He turned and looked down the bar, not about to risk her seeing into his eyes now. She knew exactly what he did. Or rather, what he was pretending to do. This was going to feel silly. But he had to answer or give the game away.

"I work at a guest ranch not too far from here," he said, staring off into space. "I'm a hand on the ranch. I do some wrangling, some cattle handling."

"You're a cowboy," she said firmly.

He glanced at her quickly, then away. "Yes, I am."

She studied his profile. He was tough and hard enough to be a cowboy, but there was so much more in his face, in his eyes. It made her wonder about him. Her gaze dropped to his hands. They were square, hard, and callused, but clean and long fingered. He might have been an artist, a conductor, a surgeon. But instead, he herded cows around. It didn't add up.

"Do you like it?" she asked idly.

"Most of it." An imp pushed its way into his smile and he didn't resist it. Glancing at her sideways, he went on. "Working the cattle is okay, and so is working with the horses. But like I said, the place is a guest ranch. And sometimes the guests can be difficult."

She looked at him sharply. "Oh?" she said coolly. "How so?"

He stretched back on the stool. "We have a woman staying with us right now—case in point. She's a real beauty, but she's too rich for her own good, and it's spoiled her rotten."

Hailey had to fight to stifle the protest that was struggling up her throat. Why, the mean, awful jerk! How dare he?

"Oh?" she said, her voice choked. "And just how do you know that?"

He gave a careless shrug. "That's no problem. It's written all over her. She has the air of command, Queen of England style. You know what I mean? She thinks everyone within earshot should be tickled pink to do any little chore she might have up her sleeve."

"No kidding?" What a lie! She did nothing of the sort. Outrage shivered through her but she hid it, digging her nails into her palms and biting her lip. "Maybe...maybe she's just lonely," she said stiffly.

"Lonely? How could she be lonely? She's got bodyguards and the house staff and—"

"Maybe she's bored stiff, ever think of that?" She knew she was getting too emotional, but she couldn't stop herself now. She went on, eyes flashing. "Maybe instead of condemning her, you might try talking to her a little, getting to know her..."

"Hey, you're sure defensive about this." He frowned. He was carrying this too far and he knew it. It was time to back off. "Do you know her or something?"

"No." She reined herself in, though it took a major effort. Sitting back, she avoided his gaze. "No, of course not. But...well, I just have a feeling you're not giving her a chance." She took a long drink of her iced tea and stared at the mirror behind the bar.

"She's had anything she wants all her life," Mitch said gruffly, and suddenly he felt the gulf between them keenly. After all, his background was very different. He'd had to fight for life itself at one point. To him, life was a struggle that never seemed to end. He could hardly imagine it any other way. "She doesn't need for me to give her anything," he added coolly.

Oh yes she does. But she only thought it, didn't say it aloud. She knew this was getting nowhere, fast, and this entire conversation was ridiculous. She had to go before she did something she would regret and ended up getting both herself and Jen into trouble. Why had she come here to sit with him, anyway? She pushed her drink away and looked about the bar.

"Well, whatever," she said lightly. "I guess what I'd really like to do now is go home."

"I'll take you," he offered, though he knew she would have to refuse. And if she didn't? Then he was in big trouble.

But she didn't disappoint him.

"Oh, no thanks," she said quickly. "I . . . I came with someone and I'd better go back with her."

"Okay." He downed the last of his drink. It went down like fire, burning all the way, and that was exactly what he needed right now. Punishment. Something to tell him he was breaking the rules. They were his own rules, but they were good rules, and he knew breaking them was asking for trouble. The sooner she left, the better.

She was gathering her things together. In another moment, she would be gone. He practically held his breath.

She slid down off the stool and looked toward where the band was still playing its heart out. Then she looked back at him. She knew she should go. She should leave him behind and hope she never met up with him again. Just a word, just a few steps, and it would be over. It would be a relief, really. Better to get it over with. She opened her mouth to say goodbye, and instead, something else came out, something she hadn't planned, and she was as surprised to hear it as he was.

"Have you been out to see the wishing well?" she asked him.

He looked into her deep green eyes and shook his head, feeling like a drowning man. She was supposed to leave, not extend this evening. Didn't she get it? Didn't she know she was playing with fire here?

"No," he said, his voice slightly hoarse.

Her smile seemed to light up the room. "Then come on. You've got to see it." She held out her hand as though she were going to lead him to it. "It's quite something."

He was a goner and he knew it. Like a man in a dream, he took her hand and let her lead him from the bar, out into the courtyard with its arbor and the scent of roses blooming and the soft whispers of the lovers melting into the shadows all up and down the walkway.

"There it is," she said, pointing out the wishing well with its bubbling water and shimmering lights. "Let's make a wish."

Digging into her purse, she came up with a nickel and a dime and handed the first to him. Closing her eyes, she paused for a moment of reflection, then tossed the coin into the water.

He watched her, amused. "What did you wish for?" he asked.

"I'm wishing for an honest man," she said with a sigh.

He laughed, not sure whether to take that as a personal insult or not. "What do you need one of those for?"

She shrugged, leaning forward with her elbows on the railing. "I just think it would be interesting. It's sort of an ideal I've always had."

He leaned beside her, looking into the water and at the colored lights set deep beneath the waterfall. "How would you even know if he was really honest or not?" he asked.

She squinted thoughtfully. "I think I would be able to tell. There would be something about him ... something ..."

"Something honest."

Turning toward him, she laughed. "Right. Exactly."

"And how about you?" he asked, leaning to the side so that he could look at her. "Are you honest enough for an honest man?"

She smiled sadly and shook her head. "No, of course not. You've got me there. But that doesn't mean I don't want one." Hugging her arms in close about her, she looked into the water. "A girl can dream, can't she?" she said softly. Then she turned and looked at the nickel still residing in his hand.

"Well, come on, your turn."

He hesitated, then tossed the coin in and watched the ripples it created.

"What did you wish for?" she asked.

He looked at her, his eyes dark in the lamplight. "It's a secret," he said.

"Oh." She shivered, pretty sure she didn't really want to know what his wish was. "I guess that's allowed."

He settled back again, not saying anything. The two of them leaned side by side, shoulders touching, and watched as the water cascaded past the lights. It was very dark where they were standing, the darkness almost like a mist, like a perfumed web tying them together. He sensed her beside him, even though he wasn't looking at her. He could feel the outline of her body, feel the porcelain perfection of her features. And this time, he didn't push the feeling away.

But he did wonder if she was feeling it, too.

"Oh my," Hailey said softly at last.

He glanced at her, resisting the overwhelming instinct to reach out and touch her hair. "What is it?"

She smiled, looking up and down the walk, listening to the whispered sounds of the lovers. "I was just thinking," she said softly, moving closer to him so no one else would hear, "about all the lies that must have been told under this arbor."

He laughed, throwing his head back. "Lies, huh? You are cynical, aren't you?"

"No, I'm not cynical at all. I'm just realistic. But I do think these places are like traps. I mean, they make it so pretty and so romantic and every young girl who's in love wants to come out here and be lied to... and be kissed."

He turned, leaning on one elbow only and facing her. "Do you want to be kissed?" he asked her simply, his dark blue eyes deeper than the shadows.

She glanced at him and then away. "I've been, thanks," she said, though he thought he could hear a slight edge of growing excitement in her voice.

"Oh, I see," he said, his voice very low. "Once was enough, was it?"

She nodded. "Just about. I'll admit I did give it a few more tries, but the result was the same."

"You know what that tells me?" He had her shoulders in hand now, holding her gently but inexorably in his control. He knew he was crossing the line, walking right off the cliff, but it was too late to turn around now. "It's been much too long since you've tried it."

She stared up at him, not resisting, not wanting to resist, fascinated by how full and soft his lips looked all of a sudden, by how fast her heart was beating. "Do you really think so?" she said faintly.

"Yes, I do," he murmured as he bent to find her mouth with his.

She'd let this happen, but she didn't know why. Maybe it was because she wasn't really Hailey Kingston tonight. Hailey Kingston didn't kiss strange men on the first night she knew them. Lately, Hailey Kingston didn't kiss anyone at all. She'd found it only complicated things to let most men get that far. They always seemed to think it an invitation to push for more things, things she never, ever gave away.

But here she was, kissing Mitch Harper. His mouth was hot and tasted slightly of the drink he'd had at the bar. She opened, letting him inside, and he came to her with a sudden surge of urgency that took her breath away. His hands still held her shoulders, never moved from them, but his fingers tightened and his kiss deepened and became so intimate, she felt as though his hands had moved, felt as though they were caressing her, finding every curve, every fascinating, sensitive hiding place. Awareness of her surroundings fell away. All she knew was his heat, his maleness, his wonderful taste.

When he pulled back, she swayed against him, smiling up at him mistily. Reaching up, she pressed her palm to the plane of his hard cheek. "Lie to me again, please," she whispered.

Her request was irresistible, and he didn't hesitate. He kissed her again and again, hungrily, intensely, not stopping to breathe, and she kissed him back, letting instinct take over for caution, leaning toward him until her slim body met his hard, muscular frame and snuggled against it, her breasts pressing against his hard chest, her senses tingling with the feel of him.

He felt her against him, wanted more of her, though he knew this was crazy, that he was insane to let it happen. But she was too good to pass up, sweet and spicy and warm and sexy as any woman he'd ever touched. And if he didn't watch out, he would let this get out of hand. He was still in control, still strong enough not to let things unravel completely. But he knew that couldn't last much longer.

Reluctantly he pulled away again, breathing hard, wanting her as he hadn't wanted a woman in a long, long time. She kept her eyes closed for a moment after he'd drawn back, as though savoring the feel of him. And when she opened them and looked at him, she smiled.

"Well, I guess this means we have to say goodbye," she said with a sigh, slowly disentangling herself from his arms.

"Why is that?" he asked, only half hearing her, still working on that control he prided himself in.

"Don't you get it?" She straightened her skirt. "It's happened—just as I warned you. You like me too much." She gave him a sad smile. "I think I already explained my philosophy."

He stared at her. "You mean about not dating men who like you? You can't be serious."

"Oh, but I am." She turned and began to walk away. "Goodbye, cowboy," she called back as she went. "It's been fun."

She could feel his anger and frustration burning like a laser into her back as she went. But what could she say? She'd warned him. And now it was time to find her pumpkin and get out of here.

It was too bad, but it was for the best. Even putting aside her own personal rules for herself, it was all just too complicated. There were too many strings attached, too many pitfalls waiting to bring on disaster—not the least of which were the lies they'd been telling each other. She wasn't planning to tell Jen about her encounter with a hand from the ranch. If Jen hadn't seen him, so much the better.

She'd wanted one fun, special night and that was exactly what she'd had. She couldn't complain. And yet, the very parameters of her evening made it impossible to build on. It was by itself, very much alone, very isolated from the world of reality. She was going to have to avoid Mitch Harper at the ranch. She didn't want him to know she, the generic spoiled rich girl, had been there, had been the one he'd kissed. She didn't want anyone to know. That way, it couldn't be ruined and she would have it forever in her memory.

She stopped for a moment, standing in the shadows, one hand against the wall, and closed her eyes, remembering how he'd felt. He was very good at this kissing stuff. Much too good, probably. Something told her she was going to have to look long and hard before she found anyone any better.

"I won't forget you, cowboy," she whispered, opening her eyes again and beginning to look around the room for Jen. "But I hope to God you do forget me."

Four

Hailey awoke the next morning with a smile on her face. It was the first time in weeks she'd greeted the sun in such a good mood.

"This is more like it," she said to her ceiling, stretching out her arms and yawning.

She liked being happy. She was basically a happy person with a fairly bubbly personality. That effervescence had been damped quite a bit in recent days, but now she felt more like herself.

"And I owe it all to lies and duplicity," she murmured sleepily.

Slowly the events of the past evening came back to her and she laughed softly. What a crazy night. Would Mitch ever realize who she really was? She would have to do her best to avoid him and hope he didn't have a sudden revelation. She was afraid that seeing him here would bring it all out into the open. How could he possibly ignore the resemblance between her and the girl at the dance? How could he not realize she was the same person he'd kissed the night before? The funny thing was, he'd never asked her what her name was. Of course, she'd never asked him for his, either. But then, she already knew it, didn't she?

Rising, she took a long, warm shower, letting the water cascade over her as though cleansing away the night before and getting back to normal. And normal, for her, was life without a man. She'd known for years that this was how it had to be. It was fun to take an excursion into dating-land every now and then, but she knew she couldn't stay there. It was just too risky.

Still, she thought as she toweled off and returned to the bedroom, it had been a lot of fun, a nice respite from this boring grind. Now what was she going to do to keep herself from going stir-crazy?

Her gaze strayed to the pink invitation stuck into the edge of her mirror. Ah, yes, Sara's baby shower. She was definitely looking forward to that. The event was only a few days away. The trial might be over by then, and in that case, there would be no problem. On the other hand, it might not. And then, she was going to have to take action of some sort. Just exactly what, she hadn't decided. Best to wait and see if it was really going to be necessary to go to extremes.

If only there was some way she could find out how the trial was going. They were keeping everything from her, newspapers, magazines, television. She thought this was going a little overboard and she said as much to Artie, the older of her two bodyguards, but he'd been adamant.

"Your daddy said no communications with the outside world, and I mean to stick to what your daddy said."

"We're just following orders, miss," his partner, Bill, had chimed in. "Don't blame us."

She'd thrown up her hands in mock frustration. "For all I know, Martians have landed and taken over the White House," she complained. "I am living in total ignorance."

"Don't worry, miss," Artie assured her kindly. "If Martians do land, I'll be sure to let you know."

"Gee, thanks," she'd responded sardonically, but it turned out to have been the wrong subject to have brought up.

"There were some the other night, you know," Artie had confided. "I wasn't going to tell you. I figured, why get you all upset when there wasn't anything you could do about it."

Hailey blinked at him. "Were some what?" she asked suspiciously.

"Martians," he'd whispered after first looking from right to left to make sure no one was listening. "A UFO."

"A UFO?" she'd cried, and he'd sprung toward her, waving wildly and shushing her.

"No, don't say that so loud," he told her anxiously. "We don't want to get the staff all riled, now do we?"

She gave him a tenuous smile, backing away. "Nooo. No riling here," she'd muttered.

"Good." He'd sidled closer. "Don't tell Bill I told you, okay? He always kids me about having a special sense for these things."

"Ah." She nodded wisely. "So that's it, is it?"

"Yes." He sighed, obviously having a hard time bearing the burden of all this extrasensory perception he was carrying with him. "I took a few potshots at one of them the other night."

"The...uh...the spaceship thing?"

He nodded earnestly. "It was green and it hovered over the house, I swear to God, and there was no way I was going to let a spaceship come down and do anything to you."

"Uh...what, exactly, did you think it might do?"

"Oh, who knows. Don't you ever watch the talk shows on TV? There've been plenty of eyewitness accounts of people being scooped up by spaceships. Then they run all kinds of tests on you before they put you back down." He nodded, going on with lip-smacking relish. "Stick needles in you and suck out information."

"Ugh." She shuddered involuntarily.

"There, you see?" He smiled, pleased that she seemed to understand these things. "It wouldn't be nice at all. And I didn't want that happening to you."

"No, of course not." She smiled at him, trying to look grateful. "Well, I have to thank you for saving me from all that, I guess."

The poor man actually blushed. "Ah, it was nothing. Anybody would have done the same for someone as pretty and nice as you, Miss Kingston."

"Yes." At a loss for words, she merely smiled as he left the room.

She'd had a little anxiety about Artie's stability at that point. After all, if the man was actually shooting at things that went bump and whir in the night, he might be a danger to them all. And so she had some thoughts about getting someone to contact the agency he worked for to ask that they check him out. But he hadn't brought it up again and there was no evidence that he really was trigger-happy, so those concerns had pretty much faded away by now.

That had been almost a week ago. The wait was getting to be so long. Surely the trial was winding down by now. She felt she'd done her part at any rate. Actually she was pretty sure she'd gone above and beyond. And she had definitely decided—no matter what, she was going to get to Sara's baby shower.

"No matter what," she said aloud, looking at the invitation again. At this point, it was something to look forward to.

In the meantime, she might as well take advantage of what this ranch had to offer. Turning, she looked at the tired little black mop on her dresser. Picking it up, she twirled it on her forefinger. "My disguise," she murmured, shaking her head. She wouldn't be using that again. Pulling open a drawer, she stuffed it inside, then turned and started downstairs. It was time she got into the day.

First things first. She stopped in the breakfast room for a quick cup of coffee. There was no one about and, after a moment or two, she made a detour through the kitchen, hoping to find Jen, but the place was empty, as well. A cursory glance about the room didn't yield Jen, but did come up with something else. There, on a shelf above the cutting board, was a newspaper.

Hailey gave a quick look about. There was no one to see, no one to censor. Moving quickly, she grabbed the newspaper and tucked it under her arm, then made her way to the back staircase, took it two steps at a time, and ended up in her room, leaning on the door she'd just slammed against the world, laughing and trying to catch her breath at the same time.

This was crazy. She'd just stolen a newspaper, and her heart was beating as though it were a major crime. And it was!

Greedily she plopped down onto the bed and began to devour the news. San Francisco was still there, it seemed. Los Angeles was reeling from an airline strike and there were peace talks in the Middle East. A major movie star was getting married for the sixth time. "Why do these people bother to get married?" she fretted aloud as she read it. She supposed hope sprang eternal and all that, but it did seem a waste of time and resources. Reading on, she found that a star was leaving a hit television show, a congressman was being indicted for mail fraud, and the president had made a speech on family values. She examined the paper from front to back, and she could find nothing about the trial her father was involved with.

Disappointed, she sneaked the paper back down and left it just outside the door to the kitchen, where she could hear the cook and a kitchen worker talking as they cleaned up from breakfast. She'd turned to go back upstairs when the housekeeper, Mrs. Arnold, called to her.

"Telephone, Miss Kingston. Would you like to take it in the library?"

A telephone call? For just a moment, she was stunned. She wasn't supposed to get telephone calls. Then she ran for the library, eager to see who was breaking the rules by calling her.

"Hello?" she said.

"Miss Kingston?"

She didn't recognize the voice on the other end of the line. Hesitantly, she answered, "This is she."

"Miss Kingston, I'm Herb Shrapner, your father's lawyer. Your father asked me to call and see how you were doing."

At last! This had to be it. Half of her mind was already planning her trip home as she answered. "I'm fine. But tell me, how is the trial going? Is it over yet?"

"No, I'm afraid not."

Her heart fell and she sighed. "Why is it lasting so long?"

"There have been complications, things I can't go into over the telephone. In fact, there are some things you might be able to help us with, Miss Kingston."

She would help do anything to get this wait over with. "Really? What sort of things?"

"I'd like to come out there and visit with you on Thursday. I can tell you about them then."

"Oh." This was very strange. No one was supposed to know she was here. Well, she supposed her father's lawyer would know, but why did he want to come and visit her? "Can't Daddy come, too?"

"No, I'm afraid not."

An icy premonition slithered down her spine and her fingers tightened on the receiver. "There's nothing wrong with my father, is there?"

"No, no, don't think that for a moment. He's in perfect health. But there are some aspects of the case I feel should be discussed with you. So I'll be out to see you on Thursday. First thing in the morning. Say about eight?"

"Fine. I'll be expecting you."

She hung up slowly, not sure she liked this development. There was something odd about this man, something that didn't feel right. Thursday was the day after tomorrow. She really didn't have to worry about it until then, did she?

Back in her room, she came up with the clothes for her usual early morning ride. Then she was off to the stables, hurrying so that she could beat her bodyguards and maybe get away from them for once.

The morning air was fresh and crisp. The stables were kept in a large, modern building, very clean and very efficiently organized. She walked down the ramp to where Blue was kept, the large, frisky mare she liked to ride.

"Hello, girl," she said, stroking the velvet nose. "Would you like to go out riding with me today?"

The horse pricked her ears forward, but remained otherwise mute. It was anyone's guess as to whether she really wanted to go or not.

"But you have to," Hailey murmured to her, still stroking. "It's your job."

Blue didn't say a word and Hailey smiled at her. Blue was not a particularly garrulous horse, but that was okay. Hailey wasn't looking for animal communications today, anyway.

She heard someone coming down the ramp, his boots hitting the wood sharply, and she figured it was the cowboy who was usually around and helped her saddle Blue most mornings. Giving Blue one more pat, she turned to greet him, but the smile of welcome stuck in her throat when her eyes met the sparkling blue gaze of Mitch Harper. Just the man she didn't want to see.

Oh no. The words echoed through her head though she didn't say them aloud. But her eyes did widen, and she stood very still, as though expecting a blow of some sort. What she actually expected was recognition. She expected his eyes to narrow and his jaw to turn to stone and his tone to be accusatory.

But that wasn't what happened at all. Stopping just a few feet short of where she stood, he gazed at her, head to the side. There was no laughter in his eyes as there had been the night before. There was no sense of sensual attraction such as she'd felt so strongly when they'd been this close. This could have been a direct continuation of the encounter of the previous afternoon, where he had reluctantly helped her move her easel.

"Well, if it isn't the busy Miss Kingston," he said, his tone wry, as he turned to put down the large, heavy canvas bag he was carrying. "Tell me, milady," he went on without looking back at her. "How does your garden grow?"

She frowned at him. She was finding it more and more difficult to believe he didn't realize she was the same woman he'd flirted with the night before. Still, even if he didn't, it didn't give him the right to be antagonistic. "Quite nicely, thank you," she snapped back. "Only it's horses I'm dealing with here, not cockleshells. And I'd like this one saddled, please."

He turned slowly and looked at her, not a hint of emotion showing in his blue eyes. "As you wish. I am but your humble servant."

She felt herself flush and wished she could hide it. "Cut that out," she muttered, stroking Blue's nose again.

"Cut what out?" he asked guilelessly, turning toward the saddle rack.

She watched him swing a saddle down effortlessly from the top rung, his muscles rippling just under the thin shirt. The saddle was a nice one, just the right size for her, just the right style. He picked well. But that didn't mean he didn't deserve a reprimand. She remembered what he'd said about her the night before. Spoiled rich girl, was she?

"You know very well what," she said coolly. "You're making fun of me."

His eyes widened, all innocence. "Not at all. I'm only treating you as you deserve to be treated." Shoving open the door into the stall, he tossed the saddle onto Blue's back and began strapping it on. "You're our honored guest. It's my job to make you happy."

She gazed at him suspiciously. The mocking tone he was using cut like a knife.

"It wasn't your job yesterday," she reminded him. "You made that very clear."

But yesterday he was working out on the ranch. Today he was here. "What are you doing here, anyway?" She glanced up and down the length of the building. "There's usually a different man here."

He nodded, pulling the bridle into place and tightening it. "Well, you see, I was late to the branding shed yesterday," he said slowly, not looking at her. "And the foreman didn't take kindly to it. He transferred me here to the stables for a few days. Just to remind me that when he says he wants me somewhere at a certain time, he doesn't mean half an hour later."

She stopped dead, feeling cold, staring at him with wide, darkened eyes. "You're kidding. I got you in trouble?"

He tested the straps carefully before turning to face her. "It wasn't your fault," he told her, gazing down at her from under lowered lids. "I could have ridden off and left you standing there. It was my choice to stop and help you."

She stared up at him and swallowed hard, not really hearing him any longer. There was a buzzing in her ears, and a prickling in her blood. She blinked, confused for a moment until she realized what it had to be. She was sexually attracted to this man.

This didn't happen to her. She caught her breath and blinked quickly, trying to steady herself. What was it, his hard biceps, barely visible beneath the rolled up sleeves of the shirt? His deep blue eyes, so knowing, so scornful? The hard slash of a mouth that had looked so soft last night and felt so hot?

"Are you okay?" he asked, giving her a bemused frown. "You look like a sick sheep."

Her mouth dropped open at the offensiveness of his statement and her sense of reason flooded back. Of all the arrogant jerks she'd ever met, why on earth was she attracted to this one?

"Guilt," she cried out emphatically, tossing her head, her eyes blazing. "What you see is guilt. I'm feeling badly about getting you in trouble, and you throw insults at me."

"That's a relief," he muttered. "I thought for a moment I was going to have to perform the Heimlich on you or something."

Grabbing the reins, he began to lead Blue out of her comfortable stable into the cool morning air.

A seething Hailey followed, alternately plotting his murder and wishing she could think of something devastating to insult him with. But as she watched him with the horse, watched his gentle hands and the way he leaned in toward the animal and soothed it, her anger faded. And though she silently called herself a wimp, she had to admit she still felt guilt over having caused him trouble. Stopped before him, she gazed up into his face, her eyes wary but questioning.

"Do you want me to say something to your boss?" she asked. "About yesterday?"

His smile was frosty as he steadied the big horse. "No, milady. I don't need you to run interference for me."

Anger flared in her heart. "Will you please stop calling me that?" she cried, though she knew that losing her temper meant he won this game.

He gave her a mock bow. "As you wish, ma'am."

"Don't call me that, either. My name is Hailey. Use it."

"As you wish, Miss Hailey."

Exasperated, she swung up onto the horse's back without the assistance he stepped forward to give her. It was touch and go for a moment as to whether she would actually make it, but pure willpower had its way, and she settled into the saddle, forcing back the inclination to breathe hard from the effort. Staring down at him, she thought she saw the laughter in his eyes for a moment, but when she looked again, it was gone. And just as well. She was completely annoyed with him now. She didn't want to like him.

And he seemed to feel the same way. Without waiting for a sign from her, he reached out and gave the horse a sharp pat on the hindquarter, and she was off, barely holding on until she regained her balance.

"Damn you, Mitch Harper," she muttered as she struggled to get control of the horse. But when she looked back, he was nowhere to be seen.

What she did see were Artie and Bill, running for the stables. They were going to catch her. And even that, in her mind, was somehow Mitch's fault.

She had a nice, hard ride, but it wasn't as fulfilling as she'd hoped. She kept looking toward the hills, thinking how much fun it would be to explore them, if only she could get rid of her two hangers-on. "Soon, I'll do it," she promised herself. Then she turned and headed for the stables, wondering if she was going to run into Mitch again.

She hoped not. The man was provoking and insulting and infuriating—and yet she knew very well he could also be charming and sexy. Actually she preferred him mean. That way she didn't have to deal with the feelings he'd stirred the night before.

Still she wasn't sure why she was letting him get under her skin. She was never going to fall in love. She'd known that from the time she was young. Men weren't to be trusted, no matter how attractive and attentive they might seem at the moment. It never lasted. And they never told the truth.

"And if I did let myself fall in love," she said aloud to the wind that was whipping her hair back, "it wouldn't be with a man like Mitch Harper."

No, not at all. The man she might love would be quiet and contemplative, the sort who thought over every issue before he gave his opinion, maybe a college professor, or a scientist. Someone safe and sure. Not a cowboy with hard, dangerous eyes. No way.

She slid down off Blue's back once they'd made their way home, and looked around, but it was the young cowboy from the other day, Tommy, who was working the stables now. He approached bashfully and she gave him a friendly smile, calibrated just right so that he wouldn't think she was giving him encouragement, but only that she wasn't a total snob. And then she sighed as she walked away. Dealing with men was always so difficult. You had to watch your step every minute.

But as she glanced back at the stables, she knew that wasn't all her sigh had been made for. She was disappointed not to see Mitch again, wasn't she?

"No!" she said aloud, being fierce with herself. And she was so adamant she almost believed it.

Later that afternoon, Mitch pulled the truck into the parking place beside the back kitchen door and looked out at the swimming pool. Hailey was giving herself a late sunning and she wasn't alone. Larry was with her, down on one knee, making her laugh.

Mitch sat very still, watching the two of them. Hailey had on a bright pink bikini that seemed to barely cling to the pertinent areas. Sunlight turned her hair to spun gold and her tanned skin took on a glow. Mitch swallowed hard, and then something inside him seemed to cave in, as though he'd been hit hard in the solar plexus. He closed his eyes and let out a string of very dark curses, muttering them slowly, almost like a prayer. She was just so damned delicious looking, and he was, after all, only human.

"But not weak," he reminded himself aloud. No, he'd never been one to give in to temptation unless it suited his needs and objectives. And this most certainly didn't. "She's just a woman," he muttered to himself, almost snarling. "Remember that. She's just a woman."

He'd hit all the right notes that morning at the stables. He'd done his best to push her away. Hadn't he? He thought he had. He didn't know what else he could do to keep her from guessing he had a special interest in her. Most of all, he had to make sure they didn't get any closer.

Instinct told him he should get out of the truck and turn and walk away, and he actually started to do just that. But he made the mistake of looking toward the pool again, and he saw Larry reach out and push back a lock of Hailey's hair, laughing as he did it. Something hot and insistent began to pulse in his gut.

Well, he couldn't let this go on. He was in charge of the kid, after all. Like it or not, he couldn't allow Larry to get too close, either. And that was exactly what was happening.

His head swiveled, searching the landscape. Where were those incompetent bodyguards, anyway? He was going to have to call headquarters again and tell them to send out another pair. This duo just couldn't do the job. It looked as if he was going to have to take care of this little mess all by himself.

Groaning, he let himself out of the truck and began to walk toward the swimming pool.

Hailey saw him coming first. She sat up a little straighter in the chaise lounge and glanced at Larry. He was in the middle of a funny story meant to disarm her. She was somewhat amused but hardly disarmed. In fact, she was growing tired of Larry and his constant attempts to get chummy. He thought his good looks and leering attitude would win her over, but he was wrong. He wasn't her type, could never be. But she wasn't about to telegraph that to Mitch in any way. No, that was a bit of information he didn't need to know.

Mitch stopped a few feet from where they were lounging, his thumbs hooked into the wide leather belt he wore with his jeans. She glanced at him, just to check which Mitch Harper had come calling. Nope, there was no laughter in his eyes. It was the ranch hand, not the playboy, who confronted them. Her chin rose and her eyes narrowed, prepared for sparring.

"Miss Kingston," he acknowledged, tipping his hat with one finger to the brim, his eyes as cold as the steel barrel of a gun. "I hope Larry hasn't been bothering you."

"Bothering me?" she echoed, batting her long eyelashes. She had to shade her eyes to look at him, with the sun behind him, blinding her. "No, of course not. We were just having a pleasant conversation."

Larry swung around and frowned at Mitch. "Hey, I'm just taking a little break," he said defensively. "Miss Kingston looked lonely here, all by herself, and I came over to keep her company."

Mitch's mouth twisted into something that might have been considered a smile if his eyes hadn't been glittering so dangerously. "Why don't you come keep me company instead?" he suggested in a tone that made it a command.

Larry reared back, but there was a look of doubt in his eyes. Hailey thought fast and reached for her bottle of suntan lotion.

"He can't come right now," she said sweetly. "He promised to rub some lotion on my back." She met Mitch's scowl with a pretty smile. "Didn't you?" she prompted Larry.

"Uh...yeah, that's right. I sure did." Larry turned and gave him a "hey, what can I do? She loves me" shrug, then took the lotion from her and pulled open the top. "There are places she just can't reach, buddy. Somebody's got to do it for her."

"Well, that somebody isn't going to be you," Mitch said shortly, erasing the distance between them and snatching the lotion from him before he had a chance to pool some out onto the palm of his hand. "I need to get the truck unloaded. Let's go."

Larry looked downright rebellious, his gaze sullen. "Hey, that isn't my job," he protested.

"It is now," Mitch told him firmly. "You go on and take care of it." He looked at the bottle of lotion, then looked at Hailey, his eyes shadowed. Suddenly he realized what he was going to do. He hadn't planned it this way, but he couldn't resist it now that the prospect had been offered to him so blatantly. "I can handle this," he said softly, partly reassuring himself.

Her pulse gave a wild jump as she recognized what was happening. Larry was walking off, looking pouty, but she hardly noticed. Mitch was pouring out a dollop of suntan lotion into his hand and moving toward her.

"Never mind," she said quickly, twisting away and looking about desperately for her towel. "I...I don't really need it. I mean, the sun is pretty low in the sky and..."

"Hold still," he ordered, taking one shoulder in his large hand and turning her. "If you need it, you need it."

His other hand came down between her shoulder blades and began a slow, rhythmic pattern across her back, rubbing firmly, spreading a heat a hundred times hotter than anything coming out of the sky. She wanted to gasp, but she held it back. His touch was like magic. She closed her eyes, not able to resist any longer. Every inch of her skin had begun to tingle and something deep inside was doing more than that.

His hand felt huge and rough, but not too rough—just rugged enough to provoke a sensual response. His fingers worked the lotion into her skin, slipping beneath the strap of her swimsuit, then working down, down, until he'd almost reached her tailbone. She felt like a cat and she wanted to stretch beneath his hand and lose herself in the sensation. She wanted him to go on and on and . . .

But no. Her eyes snapped open. She didn't want that at all. What she wanted was for him to stop. She had to make him stop. She didn't let these things happen to her. No, never. She kept all men at an arm's length. It was so much safer that way.

But when she tried to speak, tried to tell him to get away, nothing would come. She didn't have the strength right now. She couldn't do it. Not yet. His hand was too wonderful, and her eyes were drifting shut again and she was feeling such a heavenly lethargy. . . .

"Oooh."

Her eyes flew open. Had she actually emitted that sound? It seemed so, and her cheeks filled with a hot flush that she hoped he couldn't see. She leaned her head forward just a bit more, so that her golden hair gave her a screen of protective cover.

And then it was over.

"There," he said, drawing away. "I hope that does it for you."

"Yes," she murmured, feeling like a sleepwalker, still hiding behind her hair. "Yes, that surely does."

"What?" he asked, not sure he'd heard her.

"Nothing," she said quickly, moving away from him. "Thank you very much. I...it is a hard place to reach," she added lamely, avoiding his gaze and hoping he would walk off and join Larry at the truck.

But he seemed to be in no hurry at all. Standing easily before her, he waited until she finally looked up, and then he said, "Just exactly what are your intentions with Larry?"

Her eyes widened and she stared at him, all the easy, seductive sensation evaporating into the wind. "My what?"

"Your intentions," he said, his eyes clear and assessing. "Do you want to sleep with him?"

Outrage shook its way through her and for a moment she couldn't speak. "You...you..." She steadied herself, her hands gripping the edge of the seat as though to keep from going for his throat. "What business is it of yours?" she demanded hotly when she could finally form a sentence without choking.

He shrugged, looking unconcerned and even slightly bored with it all. "None. And I don't give a damn on a personal level." His eyes narrowed. "But, you see, Larry works under me so that makes me responsible. And we were told to stay away from you." He hooked his thumbs into his belt again, cocking his head to the side arrogantly as he stared down at her. "If you want him, you can have him. But don't be so obvious about it. That'll only get him into trouble."

Anger shivered through her and she glared at him. She'd never felt so insulted in her life. She didn't think she'd ever hated a man so much before, either.

"What on earth makes you think I would want Larry? He's...he's..." She swallowed hard and calmed herself a bit. "He's not my type at all. I was just being nice to him. Believe me, it wasn't my idea for him to come over and strike up a conversation with me. I was reading." She pointed to her paperback novel as though it could vouch for her. "Not that it's any of your business," she added quickly.

"So you're just a helpless victim," he said scornfully.

"No." That was something she would never be. "But I didn't ask for his attention. That's all."

His mouth twisted cynically and he looked away, as though holding back a laugh. "Sure you did."

Her knuckles were white from the grip she held on the seat cover. The man was pond scum, there were no two ways about it.

"How can you say that?" she demanded hotly. "What have I done that would make you say such a thing?"

He shook his head as though he just couldn't grasp what her problem was in seeing this clearly.

"How can you walk around like that," he noted, gesturing toward where she sat in her swimsuit, "and not think you're going to have men falling all over themselves to get to you?"

It was obvious the man was a chauvinist caveman who didn't have a clue.

"I don't know what you're talking about," she told him icily. "This is a guest ranch. I'm relaxing."

"Like that?" He waved a hand toward her again. "Sure, it's your right to do it. But when you do it, you get what you ask for. With a man like Larry, it's like waving a fish at a seal. The guy's Pavlovian. You flaunt your half-naked body in front of him in that tiny bikini and he goes into overdrive."

"Half-naked . . . ?" She looked down at her suit. It was a two-piece, but hardly immodest. It didn't show a thing it wasn't supposed to. Her belly button was barely revealed for Pete's sake. "It's a very modest suit."

That wasn't the way it seemed to him, but he winced when he tried to look at it objectively, as though he were trying to stare into the heart of the sun.

"Modest, huh?" he growled. "Maybe if you had a modest body to go with it, that would work. But with your assets, a guy doesn't have a chance."

She was calming down now, and beginning to feel an undercurrent of something else going on here. "Are you trying to tell me that men are mere slaves to their raging hormones? That they just can't help it?"

"Some men are," he told her seriously. "Some men have to be protected from themselves. And from women who might exploit their naiveté."

She stared at him for a moment as his statement sank in, then burst out laughing. Now he had gone too far and stepped over the line of sanity. "Larry? Naive? Oh, give me a break!"

But Mitch didn't back down. "Of course he's naive. He lives life on a very elemental level. If a woman smiles at him, he thinks he's in love. Don't take advantage of that."

She shook her head, exasperated with him as usual. "Listen. I don't know what planet you're living on, but we don't seem to speak the same language. I don't know, maybe you're one of Artie's Martians. If you want me to stay away from Larry, that's fine with me. Just tell him to stop following me all over the place. Okay?" Her sparkling green eyes met his blue gaze and she lifted her chin, challenging him. "And while you're at it, you could keep your distance, as well," she suggested tartly.

He gave her one of his rare smiles. "Don't worry about me, Miss Kingston. I'm neither naive, nor a slave to my hormones."

"Congratulations," she said coldly. "We should see if we could dig up a medal for you."

His grin was more knowing than she would have liked. "I don't need a medal. My life gives me all the rewards I can use."

For just a moment, his gaze swept over her, taking in everything from her red lips to the curve of her breasts and the long, shapely length of her tanned legs. "Have a nice afternoon, Miss Kingston," he said softly, turning away. "And sweet dreams. I know I'll have them."

He sauntered off toward the truck while Hailey contemplated throwing her book at his head. The man made her want to spit nails. Sweet dreams, indeed! Somehow Mitch Harper, when he was acting like this, had a knack for making her feel like a floozy.

"Or maybe a floozy-wanna-be," she muttered to herself as she attempted to settle back and relax in the lounge chair now that her every move made her self-conscious as all get-out. Whatever he thought of her, it wasn't doing much for her self-esteem. And yet, at the same time, it was providing a challenge she couldn't deny. She was going to prove her worth to this man, somehow, somewhere.

"You just wait and see, Mitch Harper," she whispered to the breeze. "You just wait and see."

Five

Mitch kept Larry working hard until after dark, and he joined right in with him, hoping the physical labor would calm him down and wipe a few things out of his mind—like the feel of her velvet skin beneath his hand, the sweetness of her mouth when he'd kissed her the night before, the flash of her emerald green eyes—the way she'd filled out that swimsuit. Chopping wood seemed like an apt exercise in raw physical effort, something that might blot out other sensations. He set himself up with a large pile and got to work, swinging an ax to smash memories, feeling the effort and the ache in his muscles as a catharsis.

But his mind wouldn't leave it alone. He knew he should never have touched her. He'd stepped over the line. The kiss had been one thing, and it had been wrong, but she'd been pretending to be someone else and he'd been pretending not to know the difference. Pretty thin, as rationalizations went, but it would do in a pinch. But this had been much worse. He'd done it deliberately. And now there were certain things that were branded into his mind, things that would never leave him. Like the way she'd moved when his hand stroked her back, the way her body had responded to his touch, that sound she'd made...

He drew his breath in hard as he remembered, and then he swung the ax and split the thick log with one blow. She would be like heaven to make love to, like no other woman he'd ever been with before. He knew it. He could sense it.

But he would never experience it. He couldn't get any closer. It would be insane to try. This was no good and he knew it. He was getting too involved.

The assignment had started out all right. He'd kept his distance and things had gone smoothly enough. Of course, he hadn't been able to find out anything along the lines the D.A.'s office was concerned with, but he'd kept an eye on her and could tell she wasn't working with secret bank accounts or visits from Swiss agents. It just might be she didn't know a thing. Not bloody likely, but possible.

In which case he was treading water and could better use his time and talents somewhere else.

He took a long ride out onto the desert in the twilight and watched the moon rise. Something was eating away at him, something that wouldn't leave him in peace. He was a competent agent and he usually tied cases up quickly and successfully. The powers that be called upon him when they had a particularly tough case to crack. It had been pure bad luck that he'd been assigned to this one. He'd just finished clearing up a major government funding scandal, where city employees were taking kickbacks from contractors. Twenty crooks had been indicted as a direct result of his work. So he'd taken a leave and gone to Hawaii to spend some time surfing the big waves on the North shore, then had come back ready for a new challenge. Instead, they'd handed him the Hailey Kingston investigation. And he hadn't balked. He'd been pretty sure he would be able to tie it up within the week and be ready for the next major operation the department might get involved in. But it hadn't happened that way.

Instead, he'd been wasting his time here and he was slowly being pulled into something he didn't want. She was just too damn beautiful for her own good. If he stayed, he was going to end up in bed with her and he knew it. The chemistry was there. She knew it, too.

He had to quit. That was all there was to it. He'd gotten too close and it was wrong. It was time he gave Donagan a call and had him send up a replacement. Turning his horse back toward the ranch, he had it all figured out. Time to get back to the real world.

He took the truck and drove on into town just to be sure, using the public telephone he'd used two days before.

"Donagan?" he said, once he'd contacted the group leader in the department. "Sorry, but I've got to bail on this one. Can you get a cavalry unit in here right away?"

Donagan's momentary silence should have warned him. "I take it this is your colorful way of requesting a replacement?" he said slowly.

"You got it. How soon can you get someone out here?"

Donagan sighed. "This is going to be a problem. We've got a rush operation brewing in Palm Springs. We're heavily committed right now."

Mitch shook his head. He'd known it. He'd stayed out here in this backwater too long. "What is it?" he asked sharply.

Donagan sighed again. "You don't want to know. It would just make you all the more unhappy with your current assignment."

Mitch groaned and slapped the flat of his hand against the side of the telephone box. "It's the gambling mob operation, isn't it? Damn. I've worked for years on the Vincent mob and when something finally breaks, I'm stuck on a dude ranch."

Donagan coughed delicately. "I told you you didn't want to know."

Mitch's grip on the receiver tightened. "Listen, get me out of here as fast as you can."

Donagan sighed. "Harper, when are you going to slow down and take life as it comes, instead of racing out to meet it halfway all the time?"

Mitch's mouth twisted in annoyance. "I like to keep busy. You know that."

"Yes, I know that."

Mitch's hand wiped across his mouth and he grimaced. He knew what Donagan was thinking. They'd had this talk before. "What are you running from, Harper?" he'd asked. "What are you trying to forget?"

That wasn't something he could explain to anyone, much less the men he worked with. It wasn't that he was running from something anyway. It was more that he had a burning need to take care of all the things that were going wrong in the world. Someone had to do it. If not him, who?

Yeah, but what drives you to it? would have been Donagan's next question. He didn't need a boss who thought like a shrink. He had no time for bull like that.

"Come on," Mitch said. "You can find someone to spell me. Do it now."

Donagan didn't answer that demand directly. "What's the problem, anyway?" he said instead.

Mitch hesitated. He hated to admit he'd screwed up. "I . . . uh . . . got a little too close to the subject."

"Uh-huh. And this is bad?" Donagan's dry sense of humor was kicking in. After all, he'd seen the subject.

"In this case, yes," Mitch said shortly, knowing he was about to get teased if he didn't play his cards close to the vest. "It's bad."

"Okay," Donagan said, amusement lacing his voice. "I'll defer to your judgment. You usually know what you're talking about. But . . . listen, Mitch. It's going to be at least forty-eight hours before I can get you out of there."

Mitch groaned. "That's no good," he said.

"Sorry. It's the best I can do." Donagan hesitated, then went on. "But since you're going to have to be there anyway, why not take advantage of the situation?"

"No." Mitch's tone brooked no argument. There was no room for compromise here, as far as he was concerned. "I don't play that game." Mitch's scorn was clear in the low gravel of his tone.

"Hey, nothing underhanded. Listen, Mitch, I didn't mean to offend you...."

"I know. Forget it." He let out a breath explosively. "Lord, I'm beginning to wonder if I died somewhere along the way and just didn't notice, and now I'm into one of the first stages of hell or something."

His outburst wasn't really meant for Donagan, and Donagan didn't have any idea of what he was talking about. Mitch Harper was a good agent, but a strange case at times. He seemed to live on an entirely different level from everyone else.

"What?" Donagan asked, though he didn't really have a whole lot of hope of finding out what Mitch was saying, even if he did hear the words again.

"Never mind." Shaking his head, Mitch got hold of his anger and lowered his voice. "Okay, I'll hang in there for another couple of days if I have to. And I'll work on the subject, see what I can do. But don't expect much. I don't think she knows a thing."

Donagan laughed, obviously relieved that Mitch was coming around. "Hey, my man, they always know something."

"I know." Mitch frowned. That was exactly what he always said himself. "But maybe not this one."

Donagan whistled on the other end of the line. "Uh-oh. You do have it bad, don't you?"

Mitch uttered a curse, said a curt goodbye and hung up the telephone. He was in no mood for jocularity now. There was no quick escape. He was stuck here.

Time to rethink. He'd been playing it stupid. He'd been trying hostility and confrontation as a device to keep her at her distance and it wasn't working. In fact, if anything, it was stoking the fire that seemed to light whenever their eyes met. It was a **tactic** that needed revising right away.

Okay. He would change. He would be courteous and friendly. Maybe that would help defuse things. Maybe. It also might make information easier to come by. He was going to have to endure two more days of this. And if he was going to have to do that, he might as well make it worth his time. He would see what he could do tomorrow. Tomorrow, as they said, was another day.

He was ready for her in the morning when she appeared at the stables for her ride. He'd been tipped off by a girl who worked in the kitchen and had worked things out with the foreman. Hailey was planning a picnic, and he was going to invite himself along.

She appeared at Blue's stall, just as he expected, carrying a basket and a saddlebag, and the two bodyguards tumbled in close on her heels. It was evident they were determined not to let her get the jump on them today.

She forthrightly met Mitch's gaze, looking cool and competent in her riding pants and short, nicely cut jacket. She'd known he would be there, known she would have to face him again. And her reaction had been a tremor of excitement that made her choke.

"Not good," she'd told herself, again. "Not good at all. He's nothing but a pompous bore who can't even recognize, the very next day, a woman he's kissed. Who needs him?"

But when she saw him, it happened again, and this time she had to be very careful to hide it from him.

"Good morning," she said, giving him a grazing glance. "I hope you're in a better mood today than you were yesterday."

"My mood is determined by events," he told her calmly.

She risked a quick look. He wasn't frowning. That was a sign of improvement. "I see. So as long as things go your way, you're happy."

"You got it." He smiled, his lips curling, his eyes shining. A real smile. "Everything would go much more smoothly in the world if they would all just take my advice.''

She gave him a double take, startled. He'd actually said that in a self-deprecating tone. Could it be? Was the Mitch Harper of the other night at the dance club rearing his handsome head her way?

She watched as he pulled down the saddle. Biting her lip, she tried to think of a test to give him. She was still smarting over the things he'd said to her by the swimming pool the previous afternoon. Turnabout was fair play, wasn't it? And maybe he would get the point.

"You were so kind to give me those helpful etiquette hints yesterday,'' she said pertly. "Now I've got some advice for you. Those tight jeans have got to go.'' She let her gaze drift down, taking a long look. "You never know when some naive girl will get the wrong idea. Just watching you might give her delusions of grandeur that are way out of whack.'' And then she waited, eyes hooded, to see if she was going to get the usual sarcastic reply.

He set the saddle down and turned slowly. She held her breath. For just a moment, he stared at her, his eyes unreadable. And then a slow grin began to crease his face. "I'll keep that in mind,'' he said lightly, his eyes dancing with amusement. "And I appreciate the concern for my welfare.''

She smiled, taking in a gulp of air, and delight scattered through her system. The playboy was back, and he had definitely taken the place of the grouch.

"Only kidding,'' she said quickly. "I like you in those jeans.''

He laughed, holding her gaze with the warmth in his. "And I like you in the swimsuit. But that doesn't mean it isn't dangerous.''

How could one simple smile make her feel so warm and comforted? She didn't know, but she liked it. Watching as he put the saddle on Blue and tightened it down, she marveled at the man. What had caused the change? Had he suddenly realized she was the same woman he'd flirted with the other night? Or was it something else? No matter. It was just nice to have him here.

He was finishing up and she had a picnic basket to maneuver. Lifting it, she carried it over to where he was still working with Blue.

"Can you figure out a way to stow this aboard for me?" she asked him.

"Don't worry," he said, straightening and taking it from her. "I'll carry it."

She blinked at him in surprise. "You?"

"Yes." His blue gaze seemed to reflect the light coming in from the morning sunbeams, and his dark hair was falling over his forehead in a very romantic way. "I'm coming along on the picnic," he said, informing, not asking.

She drew in her breath. That would provide more complications than she was sure she could handle. Besides the basic desire to keep her distance from this man, she had plans that might be ruined if he came along.

"Wait a minute—"

"Don't worry," he said, brushing off her concerns. "Orders from the boss. He told me you're planning to go wander around in the foothills, and he thinks you might need some help. That area can be pretty dangerous if you don't know your way around."

She frowned, searching his eyes. "But I have two handy-dandy bodyguards," she noted. "Maybe you hadn't noticed."

His eyes were smiling. "Yes, I've noticed, all right. And that's why he thought you might need help." He glanced down the ramp where Artie and Bill were struggling with the saddles for their horses. As she turned and looked, Bill pulled a large one down, tottered for a moment with the heavy burden in his arms, then toppled over with the saddle pinning him to the ground.

She stared for a moment, as Artie, yelling inconsequentially, got Bill back on his feet, then she looked back into Mitch's eyes. "I think I see your point," she said calmly.

And suddenly they were laughing together.

"We may have a new comedy team in the making here," she said, glancing back at the pair as they struggled to complete preparations for the ride. "Quick, call Hollywood. I get dibs on being their agent. You can be their manager. We'll all make millions."

"If we don't go crazy first," he murmured as he moved by her to take the reins. He passed very close and she let her gaze linger on the way his shirt fit, then looked away quickly. There was going to be none of that. She had to keep control, or everything would fall apart.

He began to saddle a horse for himself, a skittish gelding, and she had to think through the consequences of his coming along on the picnic. His presence might put a crimp in her plans, but what the heck. It would be fun having him along.

Fun—had she really thought that word? Dangerous would be more accurate. But she'd handled danger before. She would just have to be strong, that was all. She resigned herself to it. She would go ahead with the scenario she'd set up. If he ruined everything, so be it. He was coming along for the ride whether she liked it or not, that much was evident.

But it seemed the "boys" didn't like it much, either. Artie sidled up to her as soon as he heard about Mitch's plans and voiced his unease.

"I'm not happy about this young fella coming along," he told her, jerking his thumb toward where Mitch was completing preparations for their departure. "I don't think it's right."

Hailey gave him one of her most endearing smiles. "He's just coming with us as sort of a consultant, to help me decide where I need to go. And to make sure we all get back."

Artie didn't give her a return smile. "Well, it's not really right," he fretted. "I mean, these cowboys are not supposed to fraternize."

She held back a bubble of laughter. "Oh, don't give that a second thought. We won't fraternize at all. We may socialize a little. But fraternization . . . no, not at all." She

waved the entire concept away with a flick of her hand.
"Out of the question."

Artie's brows drew together unhappily. "You're teasing
me, Miss Kingston. But I just want you to be on your guard.
After all, I have to face your father one of these days. And
when he asks why I let his daughter get chummy with a
ranch hand, I just don't know what I'm going to say."

Hailey had a pang of conscience. It was all very easy for
her, she realized, but this man had others he had to answer
to. Maybe it wasn't fair of her to impose on his good nature
this way. Maybe she should tell Mitch to stay behind. Maybe
she should forget all about the trick she planned to play on
Artie and his partner. After all, he was just a working stiff,
an everyday joe, a nice guy who didn't deserve—

"So you just remember," Artie said, frowning fiercely.
"If he gives you any trouble at all, you give me the high
sign, and we'll have his head on a platter." He made a hand
gesture that seemed to have something to do with a guillo-
tine. "We won't countenance any shenanigans," he said
firmly, his eyes gleaming with relish. "Yessir, we'll cut the
sucker down to size."

Now that was something she would like to see—them try,
at any rate. Somehow she had a feeling things might not
turn out quite the way Artie envisioned them. Still, it might
be best to try to keep the peace.

"Now don't you worry." She made a face, slightly cha-
grined. "I promise, Artie. No shenanigans." She put up her
fingers in a Girl Scout salute.

"Well, okay then," he said grumpily. "Let's get this show
on the road."

She watched him walk back to help Bill get his saddle on
straight, and sighed. It really wasn't fair to take her boredom out on them. They were only doing their job. But she
had to do something. If she didn't, her brain would atro-
phy. And anyway, they had never caught on about the other
night. So it wasn't as though she put them into a panic all
the time.

"Just today," she whispered to herself, and turned to mount her horse.

The day was gorgeous, clear as a bell, with a few puffy white clouds scudding along the horizon. Under a sky as big as the future, they rode slowly out to meet the great outdoors, Hailey and Mitch in the front, Artie and Bill straggling along not too far behind.

They headed toward the mountains. "I want to explore the foothills," she told Mitch. "I hear there are some streams and pretty meadows and mountain caverns."

He nodded. "And some of those streams can get pretty dangerous when the mountain runoff starts," he added. "But I think I can find some good places for you."

"Good."

He glanced sideways at her and the way she sat on her horse.

"Where did you learn to ride like that?" he asked, slowing the pace of his animal and watching while she slowed hers to accommodate him.

"Girl Scout camp," she said, making the change effortlessly.

"Girl Scout camp?" he repeated skeptically. That didn't fit the image he had implanted in his mind. "Right. I'll bet you learned at whatever fancy school you went to." A picture of rolling green hills fronting dark Continental castles panned across his inner vision screen. "I'll bet they had riding masters and show rings and English saddles."

She laughed, laughed out loud, an open, spontaneous sound that almost made him join in. It was amazing what misconceptions people could have. She always thought it was funny when people assumed she had been born with a silver spoon in her mouth. It was nowhere near the truth.

"You would lose that bet, cowboy," she told him happily. "I didn't grow up rich you know."

He raised one eyebrow. "You could have fooled me."

She didn't think so. He wasn't really that easy to fool. Still, if he wanted to play this game, she was up to it. "Did it ever occur to you to look beneath surfaces?" she asked him lightly. "Do you really take everything you hear and see at face value?"

How someone with a face like hers could ask that he didn't know.

"Of course not," he said shortly, looking off toward the hills. If she only knew—it was his job to look beneath the facade. And he was usually pretty darn good at it. Somehow, with her, his instincts were faltering a bit. She had ways that seemed to blind him. But he would get over that. He had no doubt.

"So tell me about your poverty-stricken childhood."

She considered, wondering if she should go for laughs or tell the truth. Glancing at him, she thought she saw real interest in his blue eyes, and she made up her mind to skip the jokes.

"When I was a girl we lived in a walk-up flat off Union, near Chinatown," she told him.

"San Francisco?"

She nodded. "Have you been to San Francisco?" she asked.

"I'm not completely a dumb hick cowhand," he drawled, looking slightly offended. "I've been to a few places besides the desert."

She smiled. "I figured as much. I can tell you've been around. San Francisco, and maybe New York..."

He avoided her gaze and frowned. "We're talking about you, not me. Go on. I want to hear about this deprived childhood of yours." He flashed a sideways look at her. "Tell me about how you sold matches in the snow just to survive."

She rolled her eyes at him. "It doesn't snow in San Francisco," she reminded him.

He kept a rein on his smile. "No, but I'm sure you could have hitched a ride to Tahoe, just for the experience."

"Sure." She grinned and nodded. "With my matches in my hand," she added, gesturing with that very same appendage.

He chuckled, seeing her as a forlorn orphan and finding the image more appealing than he might have thought. "And only one mitten."

She shrugged, completely captivated by the scenario, seeing herself in an old-fashioned movie. "Of course. And after fainting and taking a header into a snowbank, along came the kindly priest who took me in, sat me down in front of the fire and then rubbed my freezing fingers and blew on them to keep them from getting frostbitten."

"Saved your life, that saintly man."

"Of course. And set me up with a little match shop of my own, which grew and grew..."

Mitch nodded. "And when you became rich, you built him his own cathedral."

She gave him a quizzical look. "I did?"

"Sure. Little match girls always become rich heiresses all of a sudden."

She looked puzzled, then her face cleared. "But wait a minute. Here's the problem. You don't understand something." She thumped her chest with one small fist. "*I* am not rich. My father has plenty of money, sure, but it isn't mine. I'm a normal career woman."

He gazed at her, finding it hard to believe. "You don't have enough in your trust fund to get a start on a nice little cathedral?"

"I don't have enough to get a start on a simple little dog house. I'm afraid you've been misinformed. And, I suppose, disappointed." She gave him a mischievous sideways glance. "Does this mean you'll be heading back to the ranch?"

He looked at her, surprised. "No. Why would I do that?"

She gazed toward the hills ahead. "Now that you know I don't have much money, maybe I won't be worth your time after all."

"Be serious," he grumbled, hardly giving that credence. "I'm here to guide you. I told you so."

She gave him a look of mock innocence, her eyes wide. "And you don't expect a huge tip?"

His sense of humor seemed to have vanished for some reason.

"No," he said shortly, his brow darkening, and she wished she had held her tongue. Turning his horse, he provided a guidelike gesture with his head. "Let's stop by that stream. The horses could use a drink."

They stopped and rested the horses and listened to Artie and Bill bicker, then Mitch offered Hailey a seat on a rock farther along and they sat and watched the stream roll by.

"What is it about water that seems to soothe your soul?" Hailey murmured, more to herself than anything else.

"It's eternal," he said, off the top of his head. "It's a given, a basic, like death and taxes."

She made a face. "Well, I like it anyway," she said.

He watched her for a moment before saying, "You didn't finish telling me about your father."

"I didn't?" she said, though she knew full well what he meant. "And you're really interested?"

He looked off toward the horizon, but he nodded. "I want to know how he got so rich," he said. "If he started out poor, as you tell it."

"Listen, mister. The way I tell it is the way it is." But she was laughing as she said it. "Okay. Here goes." She licked her lips and took a deep breath. It was a simple story, but there were deeper currents, things she wouldn't tell him about, that went along with it. The trick was to ignore them and stick to the surface.

"When I was very young, my father was a schoolteacher. My mother was sick all of the time and her illnesses pretty much used up whatever money he did make. Money was always going out and not much was coming in. I started early doing what I could to help. I didn't actually sell matches, but I did go door-to-door and hand out cards with my name and address, soliciting baby-sitting jobs. I started that at about twelve."

He studied her, surprised by this, almost reluctant to believe it. The image of a princess, born and raised, was fad-

ing before his eyes, and he realized, suddenly, that he was
going to miss it.

"What happened to turn that all around?" he asked.

She hesitated. "It's a long, boring story. Are you
sure...?"

"I'm sure."

She shrugged. "Okay," she said, settling back. "All those
years, despite how hard it was, my father was saving everything he possibly could in order to get his own restaurant."
She winced, remembering. Everything he possibly could,
including the money that should have gone to her mother's
medical care. But that was one of those currents she was
going to ignore, wasn't it? "He'd grown up in Chicago. His
father had been a butler in England—"

"A butler." Funny. There were those European castles
raising their hoary heads again, but this time from the
downstairs side. He shook his head, amused at himself and
his own expectations.

"Yes, a butler. They do exist, you know." She smiled at
him. "But when he came to America, he bought himself a
little pub and my father worked in it when he was young.
He'd gone to college and become a teacher to get away from
the pub, but as he got older, the dream of having his own
restaurant began to grow in him. He worked for years to
make that dream come true."

"And he did it."

She nodded. "It was wonderful. He was so good at it.
He'd been planning for years, and when he finally had his
place, he put together the perfect food, the perfect chef, the
perfect decor, the perfect marketing campaign. He was a
success right from the beginning. He has three restaurants
now, and they're all fantastically popular."

"So he's a happy man."

She couldn't hide her reaction to that. "Oh. Yes, of
course," she said faintly, but the look in her eyes belied her
words.

Mitch watched her from under lowered lashes, evaluat-
ing everything she said and the way she said it. She wasn't

going to volunteer information about what her father was into these days. And he had to wonder if she was even aware of everything. As far as he knew, Hailey's father was in trouble for providing aid and comfort to mob figures in San Francisco. But he had a feeling that Hailey didn't know about that—or didn't want to know.

They continued their ride after a few more minutes, making their way into the low, rolling foothills. Mitch led them to a cave with ancient petroglyphs, and to the site of a saber-toothed tiger excavation. Noon had arrived by then, and Hailey began to scout around for the ideal place to have a picnic lunch.

She found it near a stream, into which she deposited their drinks for cooling, and then she saw a better place farther down the slope, hidden from the water by a stand of oak, and she insisted they move to sit beneath the trees. She pulled a blue-and-white-checked tablecloth out of the basket Mitch had brought along for her, and spread it on the ground, then set out sandwiches and fruit on paper plates. But even as she unloaded, Mitch noticed that she left the saddlebag where it was on her horse, and he wondered idly what she'd brought in it.

But his mind didn't linger on it long. There were other things to think about, like the way every move Hailey made as she spread out the food seemed a gesture of elegant grace, like the sound of her laugh as she teased Artie about the possibility that Martians were watching them from the trees, like the look in her green eyes when she turned and asked him if he was hungry.

What a question. There were times, looking at her, when he felt as though he'd been starving all his life. Especially when she looked at him that way, with something smoldering down deep in the emerald sparkle of her gaze—something hot as the sun, something knowing and sensual.

Something absolutely insane. He turned his head and silently cursed himself. He had to cut this out.

Turning, he took a carrot stick and started to chew on it, vaguely listening to Artie and Bill, who had decided they liked picnics after all.

"Hey, you got any of those little bitty pickles?" Bill asked as he plopped down onto the cloth and looked at all the food with a spark of interest in his eyes.

"Look in the basket. I don't know what all the kitchen people packed," Hailey told him.

Artie sat down more reluctantly, and he stared at the sandwich with marked suspicion. "I can't eat anything with mayonnaise on it," he announced. "It gives me hives."

Bill made a rude noise. "So wipe the stuff off. Here, you want me to lick it?"

Artie jerked his plate away from the other man's reach. "Don't you touch my food!"

"Boys, boys, calm down," Hailey told them lightly. She began putting together a plate for Mitch, but she found it hard to meet his gaze. It was almost time. Could she do it?

She almost regretted her plan now. If she'd known Mitch was going to come along, and that he would be so approachable, she might have left it for another day. But when she looked toward the hills, shimmering under the noonday sun, she knew it was now or never.

Yes. I'm going to get away from them today, she told herself silently. She had to do it, for her own peace of mind, she had to prove she was still up to it, that her spirit hadn't been dulled by the boredom of it all. True, she'd escaped just a few nights before, but that had been with trickery and disguises. And with the indispensable help of Jen. This time…this time she was going to do it on her own. And just to prove a point.

She looked at the men. Each had his meal before him, each was totally absorbed in eating. The time was right.

"Oh, you know what?" she said, looking surprised. "We forgot the drinks. They're still cooling in the stream."

"I'll get them," Artie offered halfheartedly.

"No, no," she said, rising quickly. "You all have food to eat. I haven't prepared mine yet. I'll go get them."

No one looked up as she swung onto Blue and started around the oaks. As soon as she got over the crest of the hill, she shifted gears, not even pretending to aim for the stream. Leaning low against the mane, she coaxed her horse into a gallop. The wind whipped her hair and she was off. She turned Blue's head toward the hills and she rode for all she was worth.

Free!

Six

Mitch sensed something was up before Hailey disappeared from view around the oaks. There was something about the way she'd left so quietly. He threw down his sandwich, muttered something about helping her get the drinks and swung up onto his own horse, taking it easy until he hit the clearing.

There she was, racing off over the distant hill. She was going to get away if he didn't stop her.

"Damn," he muttered, shaking his head, half in annoyance, half in admiration. With no hesitation, he was after her.

His horse was bigger, faster, and he'd gained half the distance between them before Hailey realized she was being followed. She looked back, silver blond hair slashing across her face, and Mitch could have sworn he heard her cry out in frustration at the sight of him. She urged her horse on, tried to get Blue to go faster, but it was no use. Mitch had almost reached her by then.

Suddenly Blue stumbled, and Hailey knew she was losing her grip. Crying out, she began to slide from the saddle. It happened so fast, she had no way to counter the fall.

Somehow Mitch was down off his horse and in place to catch her before she hit bottom. All she knew was the feeling of falling, the quick stab of pure fear, and then the strength of his arms as he held her, the hard, solid length of his body as it cushioned her fall, softened the jolt as they both hit the ground, the sense of the horses wheeling and turning away, the perception that she was protected, saved, held by someone who valued her.

Saved. She clung to him. She'd been running from him as hard as she could go, but now... now...

Something inside was throbbing with a strange need and as his face, warm and rough and handsome, touched hers, the passion she'd had for escape became entangled with a new urgency to feel his body against hers, to find his lips and open her mouth to his exploration, welcoming him as though there were no other choice in the matter.

The kiss by the wishing well had been a revelation. This kiss took the chemistry to another level. Half-reclining on the warm sand, they clung together. The way he held her, she felt enveloped by him, overwhelmed, as though there were nothing but him, and there didn't need to be.

She wanted him in a way that swept from somewhere deep inside her, like a torrent, like a savage wind off the desert, casting aside everything in its path, flattening obstacles, tearing into defenses. It took her breath away, as though breathing were no longer necessary, as though she were giving herself up to him in some metaphysical way, merging with him, taking him in and holding him until he melted with her into a strange new being beyond description, beyond earthly needs.

Her shirt had been pulled open, exposing the flimsy lacy bra that held her breasts. His hand pushed the garment aside and took possession, fingers sliding across the nipple and curling to take it, and she arched into his touch, making a tiny sound that was half a moan, half a whimper of delight.

A hawk screamed as it circled high above them. Mitch heard it, but for a moment he'd confused the hawk with his own emotional release, and it seemed more a part of a wild and erotic dream he didn't want to wake from. She was soft in his arms, soft and round and completely arousing. Her hair smelled like honey, her mouth tasted like wine, her breath sounded thrillingly ragged against his face, and his body was coiled with readiness, wanting to take her there and then and very quickly.

But he was more than a body, more than emotions. He had a mind, and he knew it was time he used it. Slowly, reluctantly, using more self-control than he thought he possessed, he pulled away from her and looked up at the hawk.

Her fingers loosened their grip on his shirt and she blinked in the sunlight, as though coming out of a dark, delicious dream that she didn't want to end. The hawk swooped low, and she heard its wings in the wind. She lifted her face as its shadow passed and she breathed a deep, resonating sigh.

And then she looked up at Mitch and knew immediately this had been a mistake. A very big mistake. He was looking wary, as though he regretted it, too. Sitting up and pulling herself together, she tried to smile at him, tried to be casual.

"That was nothing," she said hoarsely, then coughed to clear her throat and regain a sense of equilibrium.

He looked down at her, his eyes startled. "What do you mean?" he demanded.

She took a deep breath and felt better. She was back in control, and she could almost pretend that she would never lose her head like that again.

"What just happened," she said, managing a quick smile. "I mean, that was like two bodies reacting to the pull of nature, and that is all. Pure animal instinct. It had nothing to do with up here—" she tapped a finger to her forehead "—or here." She put her hand over her heart. "So don't think it." Looking up into the sun, she gazed at him defiantly.

He stared back, amazed at her powers of rationalization. "Don't worry," he said shortly. "I didn't like it, either," he lied.

Her bright eyes flashed up to his face. "I didn't say I didn't like it," she chided softly. "I said it was nothing."

He searched her eyes for a moment, then shook his head, frowning at her. "Okay," he said gruffly. "It was nothing."

She sighed with relief. "So it's forgotten?" she asked hopefully.

His laugh was short and humorless as he vaulted to his feet and looked down at where she sat.

"No, I'm afraid it will never be forgotten," he said, and then he walked off to call the horses.

She sat where she was, watching him go. Her heart was still beating very fast and a part of her was scared. She'd never known a man like this before. She'd never felt as though control were slipping away for good.

Slipping! she scoffed to herself as she rose and dusted off her bottom. *Heck, control was escaping on a fast horse. I'm going to have to watch my step around this guy.*

She gazed at him curiously as he rounded up the horses and began back toward her. What did she really know about him? He was a ranch hand, someone who occasionally went to country dance halls and had visited San Francisco. He had, by turns, a cold, humorless side, and a warm, ingratiating side. Which side was the real man? Or were they both? And what was it about him that seemed to get under her skin?

That was the real mystery, and the danger, as well. Tall, dark and handsome were all very well, but she'd come across those attributes plenty in her life. They usually didn't do much to impress her. There was something more here, something that seemed to reach out and touch a chord in her no other man had ever found. The question was, why? And did he have a clue?

No, how could he? Surely women fell for him all the time. He would probably take it as his due. She didn't really worry too much about letting him know how he affected her. What she worried about was her own sense of balance. She knew better than to fall for the guy. But who was going to remind her body about that fact? Just looking at him—at the width of his shoulders and the slim, hard set of his hips and the way his mouth looked like a slash of steel in granite one moment, and soft and plush and vulnerable the next—made her feel all warm and a little breathless. And that wouldn't do.

What would happen if she fell for a man like that? It would be wonderful—at first. And then would come the lies, and the excuses—and the other woman he'd forgot to tell her about would show up. Oh yes, she'd been through it before. Something in her cringed, trying to keep her away from the painful area. No, she couldn't face living like that. She'd seen too much of it. It was not for her.

As he approached, she very determinedly looked toward the mountains instead of at him.

"Here you go," he said, handing her the reins to her horse. "Shall we head back now?"

She looked at him uncertainly for a moment. There was something missing from this scene, and suddenly she realized what it was.

"Aren't you going to yell at me?" she asked, her eyes narrowing suspiciously. "Aren't you going to tell me how childishly I've acted? How someone could have been hurt because of my misdeeds?"

He shook his head, frowning slightly. Her tone was mocking, but he knew there was a strain of seriousness beneath her words.

"Not at all. In fact, I can't really blame you. You're sick of being followed everywhere by those two bozos, and you're bored, so you decided to create a little excitement and get off on your own at the same time." He shrugged. "Sounds perfectly logical to me."

She stared at him for a moment, then gave him the slightest of smiles, still skeptical. "So you think you understand me, do you?" she said softly. "How refreshing."

Squaring her shoulders, she faced him with challenge in her green eyes. "And since you understand so well, you won't be all that surprised to find out I'm not going back with you," she said coolly.

His head went back and he stared at her without saying a word.

She sighed and looked away. This was the hard part. Now he was going to yell and stomp his foot and do all those things men always did to remind you they were better equipped to handle the decision making. And she was going to smile sweetly and tell him to go to hell.

But when he did speak, he surprised her again.

"I'll go with you," he said calmly. "Unless that would be as bad as having Artie and Bill along."

Her gaze flashed to his face, and she had to act quickly to avoid showing him how much pleasure his attitude gave her. He wanted to come along.

Then reality surged back and she realized what that meant. She didn't want him along. He was just too darn dangerous.

"You're not anything like having the Bumble twins along, of course," she told him, frowning. "But I don't need company. I'd like to take some time off on my own. Surely you, who understands me so well, can understand that."

She was still mocking him in her cynical fashion, but he didn't let that bother him. And he could understand what she meant just fine, but he couldn't allow it. For all he knew, this was exactly the chance she'd been waiting for, the opportunity to get away by herself and make contact with someone, or go straight to a hiding place where important documents and valuables were kept. In which case, he should give her some slack and follow her.

But he really didn't believe that was what she was up to. Her wide eyes were guileless. She wanted to be alone. That was all there was to it. Still, he couldn't let her. She wasn't used to the desert, and the desert could be cruel to those who didn't know its ways. There was no way he could let her risk getting hurt just because she wanted some quiet time.

It occurred to him for a flashing moment that it wasn't up to him, that she was a woman who could make her own decisions. But he quickly pushed that stray thought aside. Being in charge of her surveillance made him responsible for her in some dim aspect of his conscience. If she was going off into the hills, so was he.

"I can't let you do that," he told her with simple force, his gaze steady. "Sorry, Hailey, but I'm afraid you're stuck with me for the afternoon."

She hesitated, ready to fight about it. But something in his eyes stilled her anger. He had a strength about him she felt drawn to. Quickly she resigned herself to the possible and tossed away what might have been. And in so doing, she settled down. After all, she could do with a pal. As long as he behaved himself.

"Since you put it that way," she said, one eyebrow raised. "You seem to think you're making me an offer I can't refuse."

She gave him a sudden, dazzling smile when he began to protest. "Oh, can it, Mitch Harper. You can come along. Just don't start giving me orders, okay?"

He put out his huge hand and enveloped hers. "It's a deal."

She stared at the contrast made by their hands, and smiled again. "Now, let's get going," she suggested, "before Artie and Bill come looking for us."

He hesitated, looking back toward the picnic site, then shook his head. "You know they're going to spend the rest of the day searching for you."

"I know that." She made a face, exhibiting her guilt but dismissing it at the same time. "It gives them something to do. Besides, I made sure they had plenty of food and drink to tide them over. They'll be all right."

He looked at her, his face hard, his eyes knowing. "Okay," he said softly. "Let's go."

And they went.

It turned out it was lucky she had Mitch along. She didn't waste time pouting and so they got right into enjoying the day. He made things magical, showing her lonesome plains where coyotes could be seen drifting along the edges of the desert floor, and areas of painted sand and caves with the remnants of ancient civilizations on the walls, and high meadows where flowers peeked up out of thick grasses and streams meandered through, cutting the green like so many snakes, and a waterfall that slashed through a gorge in a rocky area where the water fell thirty feet and formed a perfect swimming pool beneath.

"How about it?" he asked her, a teasing gleam in his eyes. "You want to go for a swim?"

She hesitated, dropping to her knees to put a hand into the water, testing it and giving herself a chance to think at the same time. He'd been great so far. They'd explored this fascinating world like two friends, joking, kidding, not holding back a thing. Except... except the feeling that still simmered between them when their eyes met. The kind of feeling she was bound and determined to put in an early grave if she could help it.

Swimming would entail getting much too close. Much too intimate thoughts came to her. *If I take off my clothes in front of this man, we will surely make love.* And that was something she didn't want, couldn't handle. That was something that just plain wasn't going to happen.

"The water's too cold," she said, avoiding his eyes as she rose, turned from him and walked back toward the horses.

He didn't say a word but followed her, and soon they were riding again, sauntering through the countryside and chattering like pals.

"Do you love this kind of life," she asked him at one point. "Always out in the open, always free to do what you want?"

"Well..." He hesitated. In truth, he didn't live this sort of life. But he couldn't explain that to her. "It's an open sort of life, all right," he said instead. "But it's not really free. I'm just as beholden to the boss man as anybody else who works for a living."

"Yes, but you don't have to sit behind a desk or in an office or live in the city." She threw an arm out expansively. "You don't get told to stay in one place and wait. You don't feel like a forgotten item someone has let slip his mind."

He turned and grinned at her. "What's the matter, Miss Kingston? Do you feel trapped here on the ranch?"

She let out a groan of exasperation before she answered. "Will you call me Hailey? And yes, I do feel trapped. Hadn't you noticed? I don't have a lot of freedom of movement these days."

His blue-eyed gaze didn't leave her face. "You're a free woman," he said softly. "Surely you can leave anytime you want to."

She threw a quick smile his way and shook her head ruefully. "No, actually. I can't."

"Why not?"

She sighed, regretting she'd ever started the conversation down this path. There was no way she could be honest with him, and she hated lying. "I can't really explain that to you," she said evasively.

"Is it the bodyguards?" he asked. "You'd have an easy time shedding them. They're more like pesky flies than real impediments to your life."

She hesitated, looking at him and biting her lip. What could she tell him that wouldn't give away her secret? "There are stronger ties binding me than anything physical. Emotions work even better than chains, you know."

He nodded slowly, still watching every nuance in her face. "What kind of emotional ties could possibly be keeping you here?" he asked softly, really wanting to know, wanting to make her give him that much. But he could see her face close even as he spoke. She was hesitating, mulling it over, but she wasn't going to tell him.

"Oh, never mind," she said at last, shaking it off. "Tell you what. I'll race you to the fence at the edge of the highway. Last one there is a rotten egg."

He smiled as she laughed, speeding away from him, but he didn't let her win. There was no need to go that far.

As afternoon began to fade into evening, he led her to a small café at the junction of two highways, and they watered the horses and went inside. Finally, reluctantly, Hailey called the ranch to let Bill and Artie know she was all right.

The housekeeper answered, let out a shriek when she realized who it was on the line and handed the telephone to Bill.

"Hi," Hailey said, a little puzzled by the commotion she seemed to be causing. "It's me. You can call off the cops, or whatever else you've done. I'm on my way home."

"Miss Kingston! Thank God." Bill's voice quavered. "Did he hurt you?"

She made a face at the receiver. "Did who hurt me?"

"That cowboy, of course. That Mitch Harper fella."

"Oh." She laughed and looked back at the entryway where Mitch was waiting, looking very tall and rugged. "No, he didn't hurt me. In fact—"

"That's all right, Miss Kingston." Bill was whispering into the phone. "We know you can't talk with him listening. We've got someone from the local sheriff's department tracing this call and we'll have a car out to pick you up in no time. Now, how many guns does he have on him? Cough as many numbers as you know about."

She blinked and shook her head as though to clear it. "No, wait a minute—"

"We don't have much time," Bill told her excitedly. "Here's what we'll do. I'll ask you questions and you say, 'Well, I declare' for yes, and then you say, 'Is that a fact?' for no. You got that?"

This was ridiculous, but Bill seemed to be on a roller coaster that was going to be next to impossible to stop.

"Bill—" she said a bit feebly.

"Here goes." Bill was all business. "First question. Are there any other men working in cahoots with Harper? Did he have an accomplice?"

Her fingers gripped the receiver tightly. "An accomplice in what, Bill? There's been no crime. Will you listen to me?"

"You're supposed to say 'Is that a fact?'" He sounded quite put out that she wasn't following the plan. "Now don't get this mixed up. Here comes the next question."

She sighed, interrupting him firmly. "Bill, you don't understand. Mitch came along with me to make sure I didn't get hurt or lost."

"Good, good," he whispered loudly. "Just keep talking like that. It'll throw him off guard."

"Bill, I'm not kidnapped!" She said it slowly and loudly and through gritted teeth.

"That's okay, Miss Kingston. We're going to rescue you."

It was no use. She shook her head in exasperation. "Bill, I'm going to hang up now," she told him. "And I'll be back within the hour."

"No, you can't hang up!"

"Yes, I can. Goodbye."

"Wait! We don't have a trace yet!"

"Good." She plunked the receiver into its cradle and walked back to meet Mitch, her shoulders shaking with laughter.

"What's so funny?" he asked her curiously as she approached.

She thought about telling him but changed her mind. How could she ever make him understand?

"Just those two palookas who think of themselves as my guardian angels," she said lightly. "Come on, let's get something to eat. I'm famished."

They took a booth and ordered pieces of homemade cherry pie and hot cups of coffee to fend off the coming chill as the sun went behind the mountains and headed for the Pacific.

"I am so tired," Hailey said, stretching deliciously in her side of the booth. "It's been a wonderful day."

He had to agree to that, although he felt a sense of aggravation that he hadn't done things better. He was well aware of the fact that he had been with her all day and hadn't done even the most superficial digging that was going to be required to get anything out of her. From a professional point of view, he'd wasted the day. But from a personal point of view...

He cupped his hands around his steaming coffee and looked down into the depths. The best way to think of this was as another day down. One more, and Donagan should be able to relieve him. So if he could just get through tomorrow without allowing Hailey's pretty face and provocative shape to render him mindless, he should be okay.

"How much longer are you planning to stay?" he asked her. "At the ranch, I mean."

Her lips thinned and she shook her head. "Not much longer, I hope. In fact, I am definitely leaving soon. My old college roommate is having a baby shower in a few days, and there is just no way I'm going to miss that."

"Oh?" He looked up in time to catch the faraway look in her eyes. "Where is that?"

"Denver." Her smile came quickly and left just as fast. "I haven't seen her for years."

"And now she's having a baby."

She nodded. "There were four of us who roomed together in college. She's the first to actually take the plunge," she said happily. "My father has a condo in Denver. He got it when he was planning to open a restaurant there. Things fell through, but he still has the condo. I'll stay there. And I'll get in on some of the vicarious joy of motherhood. That's better than nothing, don't you think?"

He searched her eyes for a moment, wondering about her. The café was very still. They were the only two patrons at the moment, and the waitress, having served them, was in the back, watching a sitcom on television. They had the place to themselves, and they were treating it like home, flopping about casually and talking in a personal way. A ceiling fan buzzed above, and the sitcom played out in the background, the phony laughter sounding strange out here in the desert. But the scene seemed to bring them closer together.

"How about you?" he asked at last. "Do you see babies in your future?"

"Oh, sure." But she'd spoken too soon. Just as the words were leaving her lips, she realized they didn't really apply any longer. It was an intention she'd voiced for years, and she'd meant it. But it was time to get realistic. It might not apply any longer. Things hadn't worked out quite as they'd seemed they would when she was in college all those years ago. After all, if you vowed not to marry, how could you expect babies? It didn't make a lot of sense. "I mean...well, maybe," she amended lamely.

He noted the second thoughts. He'd never been known for his sensitivity, but for some reason, Hailey brought out a whole new side to him he hadn't known existed, and he saw her dilemma right away.

"It's hard for women, isn't it?" he noted. "You're more or less on a timetable."

She glanced at him, then away. Her hands clenched each other on the table in front of her, though she didn't notice. She would have said these things didn't really bother her. And she would have believed it as she said it.

"Yes," she answered, trying for a breezy tone. "For me, the point of no return is coming soon. I don't see myself going to an Italian birthing clinic in my fifties."

For the first time in his life, he felt the anguish women must go through. It was a concept he'd never dealt with before, and it gave him a sense of wonder that he could comprehend it at all.

"You never know. Technology marches on."

She gave a short gurgle of laughter. "It can march right on past me."

He studied her eyes. "You never know," he said again, softly. "You might change your mind. Under the right circumstances."

She turned her gaze his way, slightly puzzled by this interest in babies. But he seemed sincere, so she took it at face value.

"I would love to have a baby. But I'm not going to have one just to be a mother. It seems like my whole life has been like that. First I was going to be an artist. I went to art school in Paris. I was okay, but I could tell right away that I was never going to be one of the very best, no matter how hard I tried. So I came home and got into the wonderful world of retail. I'm pretty good at it. And I enjoy it. But..."

"There's something missing."

She looked up at him, surprised that he was actually listening to her ramblings, much less reacting to them. "Yes," she said softly. "Not that it's a baby," she added hastily. "But I feel the lack of something."

The words hung in the air for a long moment. Mitch looked up, shaking off the melancholy impatiently. "So find a man, get married and have a kid," he said shortly.

She looked at him and laughed. "Ah, yes, that is the masculine approach. See a problem, take out your sword and deal with the sucker. And stop whining about it. Right?"

Half cocky, half embarrassed, his crooked grin delighted her. "It works for me," he said.

She nodded, laughing, then sobered as she got back to the point. "But don't you see what I mean? I don't want deciding to have a baby to be like the other things in my life—sort of halfhearted. A day late and a dollar short. I'd always planned that when I had a baby, it was going to be because I'd fallen in love with a man who couldn't live without me, and having a baby would be a part of it all." She glanced at him, then shrugged. "And now I've decided I probably won't ever get married anyway." She frowned, pushing the whole subject away as she brushed crumbs off the table.

"Oh, forget it. I'm beginning to hear a certain whine in my voice that I don't like at all." She looked at him expectantly. "Let's talk about you."

"Let's not," he said with no hesitation at all. He had nothing to tell. Even if he could, he wouldn't be able to dredge up anything that might interest anyone. He just was. There was no rhyme or reason to his existence. And that was the way he liked it. Looking into the past only stirred up pain.

"That's not fair," Hailey said, her eyes darkening. "I've told you all kinds of things about me. It's your turn to open up a little."

"I don't have a past," he said lightly, pulling out his billfold and digging for money to pay the check. "No rags-to-riches story, no colorful family life, no year in France."

She flushed, offended. "Wait a minute. Are we back to the silly, bubbleheaded-rich-girl stereotype again?" she asked evenly, her jaw jutting out.

He put money down on the check. "Let's get going," he said without meeting her gaze.

"It's either that, or you think I made it all up."

He looked at her levelly. "Listen, Hailey. I don't talk about my past. I don't think about it, I don't remember it, I don't want to remember it. As far as your life story goes, I believe every word. Can we leave it at that?"

Not waiting for her answer, he rose and started for the door. She came behind him, feeling prickly and aware of something not quite genuine in the speech he'd just given her. It was true there was often a closed, standoffish look in his eyes. But she'd been completely candid with him—well, maybe not completely. But as candid as she dared to be. And here he was, holding it all back, not letting her get a peek at the real man she'd spent the day with. It didn't seem right, and she was fuming as they mounted the horses and started back in the twilight.

They had a long ride before them, and the horses were tired. And who knew, maybe the cops would find them before they got back. She turned in the saddle and glared at him.

"I guess I know something about you that you don't even know," she said suddenly, staring at him with satisfaction.

His mouth twisted slightly. "What's that?" he asked in a voice that told her he really didn't care.

"You're considered a kidnapper in some circles," she told him primly.

He turned and looked at her, startled. "What are you talking about?"

"Back at the ranch, they think you kidnapped me."

"What? Who thinks that?"

"Bill and Artie. They've called the cops."

He stared at her, thunderstruck, and then swore harshly. Scrutiny of this kind was something he couldn't afford. His whole modus operandi had been to lay low and keep out of the limelight. Now cops would be looking into his background. This was not good. In fact, it was just about disastrous.

She was a little taken aback by his reaction. She'd thought he'd find it a big joke, just as she had. But his face was pulled into a furious frown and he looked genuinely disturbed.

"Didn't you tell them the truth?" he demanded.

"I tried to. Bill thought I was afraid to talk because you had me in your clutches."

He shook his head as though he could hardly believe she could take this so lightly. "And you sat there and ate cherry pie and didn't warn me?" he said with disbelief. He gathered up the reins in his hand. "We wasted half an hour in there. We've got to get back."

Half embarrassed, half annoyed with him, she let out her breath in quick exasperation. "Oh, I don't know what you're making such a big deal over this for. I'll tell them the truth. Nobody's going to arrest you or anything."

"Oh yeah?" His blue eyes were cold as steel. "Maybe in your world things always come out okay with very little effort, but where I come from, I can't count on my name making everything all right. And I don't have the money to smooth my way for me, either." He turned his horse, ready to gallop across the desert. "People like me have to play by the rules. Otherwise, we end up in big trouble."

"That's just another way of calling me a spoiled rich girl, isn't it?" she said, more hurt than angry now.

He flashed her a disgusted look. "Take it any way you want to. We've got to get back before my job is gone." He wheeled the big horse and started off.

She stared after him for a moment, and to her own amazement, her lower lip was wobbling. "I'm not a spoiled rich girl," she whispered, urging Blue into a gallop to keep up with him. "No, I'm not," she said under her breath, and for just a moment, tears prickled her eyelids. "I'm just human. And I get . . . hurt when I get ignored."

But that wasn't all it was. She'd really made a mess of things and she knew it. It was true, she did tend to go off and take impulsive action without thinking of how it might affect those around her. It was a failing she acknowledged—a failing she wished she'd worked harder to overcome before this.

"I'll make it up to you," she called into the wind, but he couldn't hear her. He was racing on ahead, trying to beat the setting sun. And she raced behind him as fast as she could go.

Seven

Mitch was more angry with himself than he was with Hailey, and he knew it. He'd let the day get away from him. He hadn't thought through the consequences of heading into the hills with Hailey and now he was going to have to pay for that omission.

All in all, he'd never done such a poor job of an assignment in his life. Something seemed to keep clouding his vision, turning him from the goal. He had to get back on track and wind this thing up. He only hoped it wasn't too late. If the police were involved and making computer searches for his background, he was dead meat. It would be all over town by morning.

And then Donagan would have to let him out of here. But when he came right down to it, did he really want to go? No. And it had nothing to do with Hailey, he insisted to himself. No, it was just that he hated to leave a job half done. He'd always finished every undertaking. He wanted to finish this one as well.

He glanced back to see if she was keeping up, and then slowed his horse, knowing he was setting too fast a pace. He did want to get back as quickly as possible, in hopes of staving off the onslaught he was afraid was probably already set in motion. But he didn't have to be stupid about it. And he shouldn't take it out on her. It wasn't her fault. It was his own. He was the one who should have known better.

She caught up with him, breathing hard, just as they entered a canyon with steep sandstone sides. The hoofbeats of the horses echoed against the walls of the arroyo and the shadows were long and eerie.

She looked at him questioningly. She wanted to tell him she was sorry, but there was something forbidding about his demeanor. She hesitated, not sure she wanted to risk the reaction he might have.

"You okay?" he asked her gruffly, and she nodded.

"I'm really sorry," she said in a little voice. "I've already done enough today to get you into trouble. I didn't mean to do this, too."

The wave that swept over him was full of a feeling he didn't recognize—affection, the desire to comfort. He wanted to take her into his arms and hold her until she smiled again, and the impulse was so unfamiliar, it took him a moment to pin it down.

"Hey, it's no problem," he told her huskily. "It's not really your fault." He hesitated, wanting to say more but not knowing what to say. "We'd better get back," he said at last, turning his horse and starting off again.

She nodded and followed, feeling a little better but still angry at herself for acting like the selfish brat he thought she really was.

The ride home seemed over much too quickly. When they saw the lights of the ranch ahead, Mitch slowed. They were coming in the back way and he gestured for her to pull over before they arrived. He swung down off his horse and she did the same, turning to say goodbye.

He loomed tall and broad-shouldered in the lamplight. His face was harsh in the shadows, but not cold. She wanted to reach for him, but she held herself back.

"This has been one of the most wonderful days of my life," she told him earnestly. "I'll never forget you."

He looked startled at her honesty, and then a slow, crooked grin grew on his handsome face. "You make it all sound very final," he noted. "I don't think they'll hang me for kidnapping you. Not right away, at any rate."

"Oh, don't worry. I'll explain to them about all that. I...I just wanted you to know." Reaching out, she took his hand in hers. "Thank you," she said softly, gazing into his eyes.

He wanted to kiss her more than he'd ever wanted anything in his life. The urge was overwhelming, taking his breath away. He had to steel himself and harden his expression, just to keep her from seeing what he was going through. He was never going to kiss her again. He was going to work a whole hell of a lot harder at keeping himself in check. That was the only way he was going to get out of here with any shred of dignity left.

"Thank *you*, Hailey Kingston," he said, staring into her luminous eyes. "I had a great day, too."

She smiled, drew her hand away and turned, walking off alone, heading for the confrontation she was not looking forward to. And as she went, she was making resolutions very much like Mitch's.

"No more sexy cowboys in my life," she whispered to herself. "Not if I want to keep a tight watch on my heart."

And she definitely planned to do that.

There were two sheriff's four-wheel-drive vehicles parked at the ranch house. As she approached, she was rapidly developing a sick feeling in the pit of her stomach. She was going to have to pay for her careless attitude, wasn't she? This did not look as if it were going to be much fun.

And it wasn't. The next hour was an ordeal she hoped she would never have to face again. She had to explain everything three times before anyone would believe it, and even then, the sheriff was grumbling about records being kept and names remembered. There seemed to be something about Mitch that the sheriff was being cagey about. Bill and Artie were angry that he wouldn't share. As ex-fellow-law-enforcement officers, they felt they had a right to know. But the sheriff was closemouthed, though he gave Hailey a sharp, penetrating look whenever he had the chance.

And Hailey's feelings of guilt grew by leaps and bounds. Everyone had obviously been in an uproar—and all because she'd played hooky when she knew she shouldn't. It had been one thing to sneak out the other night when no one knew. This was very different. Looking around at all the anxious faces, she was ashamed of herself.

"Spoiled little rich girl?" she asked herself softly as all the extra people began to file out of the house. Maybe there was more to that than she'd thought when Mitch had first accused her of it.

It was after midnight when things finally settled down and the sheriff left to interrogate Mitch. Exhausted, she went to bed and slept like a log.

When she woke, the first thing she thought of was that she was going to meet with her father's lawyer today. She jumped up and showered and changed, but Herb Shrapner still beat her to the den. In fact, the housekeeper had fed him breakfast as he waited for Hailey to come down.

"Sorry I'm late," she told him apologetically. "I had rather a late night last night."

"No trouble at all," he told her. "Don't think twice."

He was an odd, thin man with gray hair and eyes that seemed to burn into everything he looked at. He gave her some very nonspecific greetings from her father and said, once again, that the trial had no end in sight.

"It's a very complex matter," he told her. "But perhaps you can help. That's why I'm here."

"I'll do anything I can," she replied doubtfully, sinking into a thick chair across from his. "But I don't know . . ."

It was papers he wanted. Her father's papers.

"But he would know much better than I where those things are kept," she told him, puzzled by his request.

He nodded solemnly. "That is our entire problem, Miss Kingston," he told her, his eyes glittering strangely. "Your father won't tell us where the papers are. We're hoping you might give us some idea of where they might be, some special place he might use to store things, some special retreat we don't know about."

He seemed to see the frown building in her eyes, and he hastily added, "Now, you understand, these are papers that could clear him. I don't know his reason to refuse us, but we think it may have something to do with protecting you. Still, how much risk would you be in if the truth came out? And your father is facing a very long sentence if . . ."

Suddenly a very sick feeling coursed through her body. There was a loud buzzing in her ears. She couldn't hear the rest of his statement. All she heard was "facing a very long sentence . . ."

"But . . . but Mr. Shrapner," she said weakly at last. "My . . . my father isn't on trial. He's just testifying."

"Is that what he told you?" The man coughed delicately behind his cupped hand. "Well, I'm sorry, my dear. But I think you'd better know the truth. If you can think of anything that might help your father . . ."

The rest of the meeting passed in a dream. Hailey was in shock. She couldn't think. He was saying things about prison cells and appeals and long waits and every concept was tangling into a terrifying mass in her mind. He was saying only she could save her father from this. And only if she came up with some papers she had never heard of before. She smiled and nodded and maintained an outer calm, but inside, she was screaming at the top of her lungs.

He'd lied to her again. Her father had lied to her again.

She said goodbye, that she'd call if she thought of anything, then smiled and shook hands and showed him out. But all the time, her mind was working frantically, trying to think, trying to sort out the conflicting stories.

"Oh, Daddy," she whispered, hugging herself as the lawyer walked toward his car. "How could you do this to me? And how am I going to save you if you never tell me the truth?"

But little by little, sanity returned. By the time the man's car was nothing but a cloud of dust in the distance, she'd had second thoughts. Why would her father's lawyer have come here and talked to her this way behind her father's back? It really didn't make much sense. And if he came here without her father's permission, how did he know where to come? Surely her father, who had been so careful about hiding her away, was not throwing out the information on her whereabouts to anyone who was interested.

And then deductive reasoning took her further. What if this man wasn't her father's lawyer at all? What if *he* were the one who was lying. What if...?

Catching her breath in her throat, she flung herself out of the house and ran toward the bunkhouse. Her first intelligent thought was that she had to find Mitch.

The bunkhouse was hardly the board-and-bunk dormitory of old. A nice, airy building, it had a comfortable common room and kitchen, and then various private rooms down a long hallway. It was still early, but all the men seemed to be gone. Disappointed, Hailey walked down the hall until she came to the door with Mitch's name on it.

She knocked without much hope, but her heart lifted when he answered, and she pushed open the door and went in.

He was just waking up, his hair mussed and falling over his forehead, his eyes slightly glazed. But when he saw her he quickly pulled the blanket up over his wide, naked chest and frowned.

"What are you doing here?" he demanded, not showing one shred of friendly hospitality.

She gazed at him, knowing she was playing with fire. He was so darn male, so attractive, she could easily lose her way if she wasn't careful. But she was going to be careful. Very, very careful. And she was going to ignore all the temptations he represented. After all, she had more important things to think about today.

"The question is, what are *you* doing here?" she countered, hands on her hips and a sparkle in her eyes. "Aren't you a little late for work?"

He looked at her for a moment, then rubbed his face with the palm of his hand, grimacing. "I was being interrogated by the sheriff until after three," he told her grumpily. "I figure I deserve a little extra sleep."

"Oh." She smiled apologetically, trying not to notice how adorably sleepy he looked. "Sorry about that. I guess that's my fault." Feeling awkward standing over him, she looked around the room for a place to sit, but the only chair was covered with his clothing from the day before, so she took the bit in her mouth and flopped down on the bed.

"Ouch," he complained, pulling his foot out from under where she sat.

"Oh. Did I hurt you?" She met his gaze and couldn't hold back a quick giggle.

And he couldn't resist an answering grin. "No, you didn't hurt me," he said, leaning back against his pillow. "It's just that I'm not used to being sat on so early in the morning."

"Wimp," she murmured.

They stared at each other until it became uncomfortable, and then he looked away and cleared his throat. "Uh, is there some reason you came barging in here to make sure I didn't get a full night's sleep?" he asked her lightly.

"Oh, yes." Suddenly she remembered why she'd come. "I have a favor to ask of you, if you think you can do it."

His eyes narrowed suspiciously. "That all depends."

"I know that." She gave him an exasperated look. "Here's the deal. My father's lawyer came for a visit this morning. And...well, I think there's something fishy going on. I want you to help me."

He stared at her, then looked away quickly so as not to reveal what he was thinking. The lawyer had shown up? Here? And he'd been sleeping? The way he'd heard it, Hailey was supposed to be such a secret that no one except her father knew where she was—and a law enforcement agency or two. What the hell was going on?

"Your father's lawyer?" he repeated slowly, as though he didn't understand at all.

"Yes, you see..." She took a deep breath. She knew she wasn't supposed to talk about this, but things had changed. She'd been alone for an awfully long time, and she needed an ally just to make sure she wasn't exaggerating things in her own mind. "My father is testifying in a trial in San Francisco. There are gangsters involved. That's why he sent me here, to be safe."

He stared at her, waiting. That wasn't quite the way he'd heard it, but close enough.

She sat very straight, her hands twisted together painfully in her lap. "I haven't had much contact with my father since I got here. Just a few letters. Now this man who says he's my father's lawyer shows up and wants me to find some old papers or something."

Damn. This was not good. Mitch groaned silently.

"What do you mean, who 'says' he's your father's lawyer? Don't you know him when you see him?"

She shook her head. "I've never seen this man before in my life. And something about him, something about the things he said, made me—" she licked her dry lips "—suspicious," she said at last, firmly and clearly.

Smart woman, he thought to himself, though he didn't say it. Now came the hard part. Whoever the man was who'd come knocking on her door, ten to one he was not her father's lawyer. This had been bound to happen and he should have seen it coming, would have if he hadn't been blinded by... certain emotions that he should have the strength to suppress. After all, he'd seen Pauly the other night at the dance club. Pauly wouldn't have been snooping around if someone hadn't been onto the general area of her hiding place.

"What did this guy look like?" he asked her quickly.

She thought for a moment. "Tall. Thin. Kind of gangly."

He nodded. At least it wasn't Pauly. But whoever it was, he was after the very same material Mitch himself was searching for. So what was he going to do, be as honest with her as she was being with him? He glanced at her for a moment, noting the sunlight on her fresh face, and felt like a heel. Not on your life. He couldn't possibly do that. This was his job, after all. But all the same, he knew he wasn't exactly being a hero.

"Did you tell him anything?" he asked, watching her face.

She shook her head. "I told him my father would know much better than I do where any papers are."

"Good." This was his cue. He should ask her himself. After all, she obviously trusted him. If she did know where the papers were, maybe she would tell him. Then he would return to the D.A. with a success instead of the failure that had been looming over his head for days. Yes, he definitely had to give it a try. He glanced at her again. Now. He had to do it now. He opened his mouth to ask her, but before he got the words out, she spoke instead.

"I'll tell you the truth," she said, gazing into his eyes with such earnestness it made him wince. "I don't think this man is my father's lawyer. And if he isn't, I don't think he's just gone away. He wants something and he's not going to give up. He's still around. Either that, or he's got someone watching me."

Ah, yes. She was a smart one and she was catching on fast. If she only knew just how many were watching. Yeah, right. If she only knew, she wouldn't be talking to him right now.

"So what I'd like you to do is go into Palm Springs for me," she said, a slight frown between her delicate brows. "I know it's a long drive, but this is important. Go to the library and see if they have a San Francisco paper. And if they do, look for stories about the trial. I'd really like to know how it's going. And look especially for pictures and make a copy of any pictures of my father's lawyer you might find. Could you do that for me?"

"Of course."

He gazed at her, impressed. But also disquieted. He had no doubt she was right. The sheriff, the night before, had hinted around that he knew more than he could say, things he'd probably come to know through looking into Mitch's background, unfortunately. But he'd said there had been inquiries about Hailey. That there had been strangers seen in town. This man who had been to see her was after things her father's lawyer wouldn't be sniffing around for. And if the mob had figured out where she was, she was going to have to be taken somewhere else.

But he couldn't get involved in that. He couldn't let her know he had anything to do with it all. Still he could help her.

"I'll go in to Palm Springs right away," he told her. "Just as soon as a certain lady gives me some privacy so I can get out of my own bed."

"Privacy?" She was teasing him now, relieved that he was going to help her, relieved that she seemed to have someone on her side. "What on earth does a big strong man like you need privacy for?" She raised a superior brow. "You should have enough confidence in yourself to do whatever you need to do regardless of who's watching."

"Oh, I do have that," he assured her, making as though to sweep back the covers.

She gave a little shriek and jumped up, lost her footing and fell right into his arms, laughing and struggling playfully.

"Hey," he said, smiling down at where he held her against his strong chest. "You're sitting on me again."

"Oh, brother." She laughed, looking up at him. "We've got to stop meeting this way. It's getting to be a very tedious habit."

"Isn't it?"

But he didn't let her go, and she really didn't try to escape. Instead, his hand went to her hair, a natural move, one he made without thinking. And when she felt it there, she shivered, more with delight than anxiety, and felt herself melting against him. His fingers flexed in her hair and she sighed, knowing all her good intentions were blowing away in the wind—and knowing that she wasn't going to be able to dredge up one moment of regret about it.

And neither was he, not for now. As she reached up to kiss him, he pulled her closer, enjoying the feel of her through the blanket, enjoying holding her against him, with only one thin blanket between her and his naked body, reveling in the sense of her slight, delicate frame against his strength.

"We shouldn't do this," he muttered at one point, but she was laughing low in her throat and reaching to pull his mouth back over hers.

She'd never been like this before. She knew it would be so easy to make love with this man. It had never been easy for her before, and she'd decided long ago that some people—namely her—weren't made for love and lovemaking. The times she'd tried had been awkward affairs, full of groping and regretting and wishing she was home in her own bed.

But this was different. This was hot and searing and urgent. She wanted him. By God, she wanted a man. And when it finally hit her just what exactly she wanted him to do, she drew back, startled by it. This wasn't supposed to happen to her, and she wasn't sure she liked the fact that she enjoyed it so much.

"Whoa," she murmured, rising and sliding off the bed, feeling dizzy and searching for her footing before going on. "I promised myself that wouldn't happen again."

"So did I," he said softly, and she turned to look at him, wondering why.

They stared at each other for a long moment, then she forced a smile and began to prepare to go.

"I suppose you think that was 'nothing' again," he noted dryly. "Come on, give me the day's rationalization so I can get with the program."

She shook her head at him and couldn't resist a quick grin. "No, I don't think that quite qualifies as 'nothing,'" she admitted. "But I'm pretty sure it might go under the heading of 'shenanigans,' which is something Artie has specifically warned me against."

He grimaced, his eyes shining. "Good old Artie," he drawled.

"Yes." She hesitated, looking at him, wondering what he would do if she flung herself back into his arms. Her heart was still beating like a drum in her chest, and she was tempted, really tempted.

He read the temptation in her eyes and groaned, gesturing toward the doorway. "Get out of here so I can get going," he told her. "I have a feeling we shouldn't let this drag on too long before we decide what we're going to do with you."

She nodded slowly, not really questioning that he would feel himself so deeply involved so quickly.

"By the way," he called after her as she went into the hallway. "What is the name of the trial I'll be looking for?"

She hesitated. "I don't really know," she admitted, and then she added something that almost broke her heart. "Maybe you should look under Kingston," she said softly, so softly he could hardly make out what she'd said. "I just don't know."

He let it go at that and listened as she walked down the hall and out of the building. She was just too damn innocent to know anything, he reasoned as he chastised himself for not asking her about the papers. She didn't know anything. She couldn't.

And at the same time he thought the words, he knew it was the kiss of death for his career. He'd never let himself get entangled like this before. How was he going to stop it when he seemed to have lost all self-control?

"Never trust anyone," he told himself aloud. And he believed it. This just seemed to be one of those times when he couldn't live it.

Eight

——

Hailey was nervous as she waited for Mitch to come back from Palm Springs. She went into the kitchen and had a small gabfest with Jen, hearing all about the blond cowboy, then went up to her room and got out the sketches she had made of Mitch a few days before, organizing them and adding a touch here and there. She'd drawn him hard and cold and sarcastic, and now she knew he wasn't like that at all. At least, not all the time. But the pictures pleased her just the same. They represented the Mitch she'd known before she really knew him. Someday she was going to have to show them to him.

Someday? What was she talking about? She had a growing sense of unease here and she was pretty sure she would be leaving soon. When she'd been in the kitchen, talking with Jen, a cowboy she'd never seen before came to the back door and her first instinct had been to stay out of sight. What if he had been hired to keep an eye on her? But she fought her fear by being friendly to the young man and talking loudly to Jen, laughing at one of her silly jokes.

"Show no fear," she counseled herself silently. "Don't let the jerks know they have you scared."

Did Mitch realize she was scared? She wasn't sure. He'd certainly gone to do her errand easily enough, with no arguing or scorn for her concern in the matter. But did he really get it? Did he know she might be in danger?

Funny. She hadn't really taken it seriously before, when her father had warned her. She'd come here to the ranch more to humor him than anything else. Finding out he'd hired Artie and Bill had given her pause, but she'd really thought he was just overreacting.

But the visit from the lawyer had suddenly brought everything into focus for her. She'd smelled a rat right away, and all of her father's warnings had come streaming back into her mind, and now she was sure he was right. The mob didn't play around. When they went after something, they generally ended up getting it. And now her carefree, lighthearted attitude—as if this were all a game—seemed pretty naive.

But how to communicate that to Mitch? She fretted, thinking she should have explained it better to him, should have told him not to be too open about the newspapers, not to tell anyone. How would he know not to do all that if no one told him? What if he came back and announced what he had obtained for her in front of exactly the wrong person? Since she had no idea who that person might be, she had to assume it was anyone and everyone.

She was watching from her bedroom window when Mitch drove into the yard. He went to the rear of the truck, took out a pile of boxes and started for the back door. She raced down the stairs to meet him.

Only Jen was in the kitchen, opening the back door to Mitch. Hailey grabbed an apple from a bowl on the counter and pretended not to care at all. Mitch glanced at her, but without anything other than a quick nod of recognition, which she returned nervously.

"Fresh vegetables," he told Jen, bringing the boxes in and putting them on the sink. "I've got a case of potatoes out there, but I'm not sure if they're the kind you wanted. Why don't you come on out and take a look?''

Always agreeable, Jen went promptly toward the door and Mitch looked back at Hailey, nodding significantly toward a box of lettuce he'd placed near her.

She waited until they were both out the door, then opened the box and found a folder full of copies stuck inside the top. Slipping it under her arm, she made a quick retreat to her room, breathing hard as she closed the door and flopped down onto the bed with the folder.

Mitch had done a wonderful job. There were clippings from the beginning of the trial to the day before. It was all here, right in front of her. Now she would know the truth.

Mitch mulled over the situation as he hauled a truckload of baled hay into the barn. He'd skimmed the press clippings as he copied them. It seemed things were pretty much as he'd suspected. Hailey's father had gotten a little too close to some pretty nasty characters, and now he was going to have to pay the price. He wasn't on trial, however. He was the chief witness for the prosecution, and unless Mitch missed his guess, a prime candidate for the witness protection program sometime real soon.

And that left Hailey out on a limb, with only the flimsiest protection herself. He paused, pressing a button and watching the bales cascade down into the holding bin while he pondered that. He was trying to figure out what had gone wrong. He'd been trying to figure that out for quite some time. He'd never fouled up a case this badly before. And he never wanted to do it again.

It wasn't that she was so beautiful. Sure, he was attracted to her. How could he help it? He was a normal male and she was one of the more stunningly exquisite examples of the female of the species. But he'd been attracted to women before and it had never turned his head and thrown him off his game this way. A lot of the cases he'd covered had involved beautiful women. But they'd been mostly beautiful wicked women, when you came right down to it.

That was one of the reasons he'd grown so cynical of late. He didn't expect, any longer, to come across someone who seemed, at least on the surface, to be about as decent as you could get.

He hated being cynical. But after the life he'd led, how could he help it? Still, he'd have to say she seemed to be as pure and innocent as any woman he'd ever met—a really good person. A diamond that had turned up in his hand when he'd thought there was nothing but fool's gold left out there.

At least, that was the way it looked, he reminded himself sharply. It wasn't that he'd never been fooled before. Too many times, in fact.

At first, he'd been pretty sure she was too good to believe. All that talk about finding an honest man—he hadn't taken it seriously. But now that he knew her better, he was beginning to realize she meant it. Too bad he wasn't an honest man himself. He'd come too far, been through too much, to call himself honest. He was a survivor, and that really didn't count, did it? He tried not to hurt anyone who didn't deserve it, but he was no saint.

So what was it that had gotten to him? That she was a good person caught up in a bad deal? Had that started his protective juices flowing? He usually only felt that deep, instinctive urge to shelter animals and small children, not fully grown women. Adults usually deserved whatever mischief they'd gotten themselves into. There were very few pure innocents left in the world. Very few who were as vulnerable to pain as...

He drew his breath in sharply and backed the truck up. He usually tried not to think about his father, about how he'd lost his way, lost his mind, after he'd lost everything he'd loved and built-up to the swindlers who turned out to be his own brothers-in-law. How Mitch, at twelve years of age, had been forced to take over and be the man of the family. That situation did not a very happy childhood make. And that was just another reason he didn't like to look into the past.

He parked the truck behind the barn and swung down out of the driver's seat, only to see Hailey coming his way, walking from the house. She wore slim jeans and a plaid shirt with the tails tied at the waist. Her hair was flowing free about her shoulders. Her step was quick, her stride graceful, and she shone with a freshness that made his pulse pound.

Swearing softly to himself, he grabbed a rope and tried to look busy, tried to turn away, but the pull of her was too strong, and he stood, helplessly watching, as she came to a stop before him. Her green eyes were full of questions. His knuckles whitened as he clenched the rope he held, watching her, waiting.

"Well?" she said expectantly.

He frowned. "Well, what?" he answered shortly, not sure he was ready for her answer.

"Did you take a look at the articles?" she asked.

"Yes. I pretty much got the picture." He shifted his weight and looked at her. "How about that lawyer? Was it the man who visited you this morning?"

She shook her head, her eyes darkening. "No. The name was the same, but the man wasn't. He was a phony."

Mitch nodded slowly. "I thought so," he muttered. Sure. When he called her the other day, he was probably checking out a lead and surprised as hell that he actually got hold of her so easily. Otherwise he would have been here sooner. This didn't look good.

She looked up at him brightly and pretended to smile, though she felt pretty desolate inside when she thought about it. She hated this, hated the suspicions, the lies. She hated that she'd doubted her father again. He hadn't filled her in the way he should have, but he hadn't lied, either. Not this time. It was the phony lawyer who had done that. The phony lawyer who was probably a front for the mob.

"I think I'd better leave," she said. "Don't you?"

He hesitated, torn. It would be good for her to get out of the mob's way. But he would feel a lot better if he was nearby in case she needed him. If she left, he would probably never see her again. And God only knows what would happen to her. Did she have anyone she would really trust? He gazed at her speculatively.

"Have you contacted your father?" he asked her.

She shook her head. "I'm not supposed to, just in case someone is tapping his phone. Besides, I don't know where he is right now. I think he's staying in a hotel somewhere near the courthouse."

She was pretty much all alone. Silently Mitch cursed the father who'd put her in this position. At the same time, he wasn't sure what he could do to help her. His assignment here was almost done, and he would have another case to go to immediately. As always.

"Tell me why your father put you here," he said.

She averted her gaze. It was always a problem to try to explain her father to others.

"He told me he wanted to be able to testify honestly," she told him slowly, "and not have to worry that the gangsters he was testifying against might get hold of me and force his hand."

He digested that for a moment, then asked her, "Did you believe him?"

Her eyes widened and she looked straight into his. What...could he read her mind or something? "Of course," she said defensively. "Why do you ask?"

His dark blue eyes glittered in the sunlight. "Does he always tell you the truth?" he asked softly.

She stared back at him defiantly, but he returned the stare, and slowly her defiance crumbled.

"No," she allowed softly. "Not always."

She'd never admitted that to another living soul, never admitted how much it hurt, how much it had distorted her life. A light flood of moisture filled her eyes and she turned away, blinking rapidly.

But not quickly enough to avoid his seeing. And once he'd seen, all his resolution evaporated and he erased the distance between them, curling her into his arms. "Hailey, listen to me," he murmured, holding her tightly. "It doesn't matter."

She blinked away the tears, determined not to cry. "What do you mean, it doesn't matter?"

For years, it had been all that mattered. Now she'd pretty much learned to live with it. But there was something in the warmth of Mitch's embrace that made it fade, made it seem unimportant. It felt so good to have him hold her. She would love to depend upon him, to stay there in his strong, protective arms and let him shield her from the mob, from her father, from everything. Let him take over, decide where she was going to go, what she was going to do, to keep the danger from the door.

But she knew she couldn't do that. She didn't really know who he was or where he came from or what he wanted with her. She couldn't trust anyone, no matter how much she wanted to. If she couldn't even trust her own father, how could she trust any man?

"Your father's problems shouldn't be yours," he said, his voice barely concealing his anger. "We'll have to figure a way to get you out of here."

She'd already come to that conclusion and she was ready. She had to go. But she had to go alone.

Slowly she drew away from him. "I'd better get back," she said, avoiding his gaze. "Artie and Bill will be coming after me."

"We'll talk later tonight," he suggested, releasing her reluctantly. "We'll go over plans then. Okay?"

She nodded, but her head was turned away.

"Okay," she said softly.

Turning sharply, she started back toward the house, walking as quickly as she could and trying not to stumble. It was hard to see her way when her eyes were brimming with tears again, but she didn't dare wipe them. Mitch mustn't see her cry.

Mitch spent the afternoon working as close to the house as he could manage. He wanted to keep an eye on who was

coming and going. There were times he had to make trips
out to the barn, or to the branding shed, but he never stayed
long. And all the time, he was mulling over what he could
do to get Hailey out of there—where she could go, what she
could do, that would keep her out of trouble.

The afternoon workers arrived, and he noted Jen's car
was gone, but other than that, life seemed to drag on nor-
mally. He had an argument with Larry, which wasn't un-
usual these days, and a short talk with the ranch foreman,
and then, as he was walking toward the bunkhouse, he noted
a rental car coming into the yard, and he stopped to see who
was arriving.

A short, square-looking cowboy got out of the car and
started walking toward him, and he knew right away this
was the man he'd been waiting for.

"You Mitch Harper?" the cowboy asked.

Mitch nodded, waiting.

"I'm Gary Samuels. Donagan sent me," the man said,
nodding but not sticking out his hand.

Mitch nodded again. "About time you got here," he
grumbled.

The man gave him a gap-toothed grin. "Yeah, I heard
you were chomping at the bit. Donagan pulled me off the
Palm Springs case to get out here and relieve you. And he's
counting on you to get back and fill in on that." He laughed
shortly. "He even let me use the agency Cessna to fly in
here, so you could use it to get back. It's at the little cow
pasture they call an airfield, just outside of town."

Mitch nodded. "Okay," he said, though his tone lacked
all sense of enthusiasm. "I'd better fill you in on what's
going on here." Looking around quickly, he made a decision. "I'll take you to meet the foreman. Come on. We can
talk in the truck."

On the way there, he gave Gary an overview, though all
the time he was thinking hard, not sure what he was going
to do. How could he go off and leave her?

Gary Samuels was here now, and he would take care of
her. He would make sure no one got to her. He would con-

tinue, however, to go after those papers. How could he not? That was what the job was. And it killed him to think of anyone, even a fellow agent, pushing her, treating her like a suspect. Especially when he himself wouldn't be here to protect her.

He left Gary with the foreman and raced back to the house, knowing all his rationalizations weren't working. They couldn't work. They stank.

He couldn't leave her here. And now he had a plane at his disposal. All he had to do was grab her and take off for Palm Springs. Then he could keep her with him while he worked on the Palm Springs case.

Well, if he was honest with himself, he knew that wasn't really going to work. But he was definitely going to take her with him. He couldn't leave her behind. He knew that as well as he knew his name.

He drove into the maintenance parking and got out, looking at the house parking lot. There were no strange cars in the area, other than the rental car Gary had arrived in. But as he turned to head for the bunkhouse, he saw Jen coming out, carrying her purse.

"Where are you going?" he asked her, frowning.

She looked up at him, surprised, and then wary. "I...uh...I'm waiting for my boyfriend to pick me up. I'm going home."

He turned and stared at the parking lot. "But your car was here earlier," he said slowly. "Wasn't it?"

"Oh. Yeah. I...uh...I let a friend borrow it."

He stared at her for a moment, his blue eyes fierce, and then he turned on his heel without another word and started for the house.

"Mitch," she called after him. "Wait." Running after him, she tried to catch up with his angry stride.

He went in through the back door and marched through the kitchen without acknowledging the cook, and Jen ran behind him anxiously.

"Mitch, wait up, let me explain."

He didn't wait. Taking the stairs two at a time, he jerked open the door to Hailey's bedroom and stormed inside, stopping in the middle of the room and turning slowly, taking it all in, while Jen stopped, panting, at the door.

"Mitch, you shouldn't be up here," she whispered loudly, looking up and down the hall as though she expected a reprimand at any moment.

He looked hard at the room. Clothes still hung in the closet. Many of Hailey's things were stacked near the dresser. But there was an air of emptiness to the place. And then he saw the packages set neatly in a row on the bed. Walking over slowly, he picked up the first one, a letter addressed to Artie and Bill. The next was an envelope for the staff. Then a letter to her father. And finally, a series of charcoal drawings, tied with a blue ribbon and addressed to Mitch.

He took his package and pulled the ribbon off, staring silently at the pictures, one at a time. Then he turned to Jen, his eyes burning.

"Where is she?" he demanded.

"I don't know," she responded defiantly.

Experience told him she was lying. His first instinct was to try torture, but he controlled himself. There were other ways to get information, ways that might not get him locked up in the end.

"Jen." He pulled her into the room and closed the door. "I've got to find her," he said, gazing into her eyes with all the earnest appeal he could muster. "I know she's scared, and she's running. And she's right to be. She may be in real danger."

Jen shook her head slowly, her eyes wide with anguish. "I don't know what you're talking about," she claimed, her voice just a little too high. "I don't know where she is. Honest."

He resisted the urge to shake her. "Yes, you do, Jen. She's in your car. Now we both know she must have told you where she was taking your car. So you might as well tell me."

She shook her head and he grimaced with annoyance, but at the same time, he saw something on the floor, near the doorway. Bending down, he picked it up. It was a card shaped like a little duck, and it had the name of the woman who was giving the baby shower Hailey had said she wouldn't miss for anything. The shower was only a few days away. Now where was it Hailey had said the shower was? Someplace where her father had a condo...

"Denver," he said aloud, turning to look at Jen. He shoved the card into his back pocket. "I'm going to Denver, Jen. Are you going to help me find her or not?"

Jen opened her mouth, then closed it again, shaking her head, in complete misery.

"She took your car, didn't she?"

She nodded slowly.

"Did she get dolled up in the black wig and uniform like the other night?" he asked harshly.

Her gaze flew to his face, stunned.

"And then she got into your car and drove off. But she's not going to try to drive all the way to Denver, is she?"

Jen shook her head, avoiding his eyes.

"Where is she leaving your car, Jen?"

"Las Vegas," she whispered, looking as though she were about to cry. "At the parking lot at the Camelot Hotel."

"Jen. Thank you." He gave her hand a quick squeeze, then gathered up his pictures and prepared to go. "Don't tell anyone else," he advised her.

"I won't," she said quickly, looking furtive. "I...I'm going to stay at my boyfriend's house. And I don't come in to work again until Monday."

"Good." He gave the room another look, then opened the door and escorted her out. "You've been a big help. And a good friend to Hailey."

"Have I?" She looked at him doubtfully. "I hope so. Oh, I really hope so."

Nine

The night was rolling by and Hailey felt as though she were racing past a graveyard with her fingers crossed. The highway was almost empty. Whenever she caught sight of headlights coming up from behind, her pulse beat more quickly and her gaze couldn't stay away from the rearview mirror. She wouldn't feel safe until she got to Las Vegas.

"If then," she muttered aloud. "If then."

But all in all, it felt good to be on the road. She felt free in a way she hadn't for a long time. Her only regret was a mixed one. She hated leaving Mitch without saying goodbye. At the same time, she knew it was better to get as far away from him as she possibly could. The feeling that had been building between them was getting much too intense. If she'd stayed any longer...if she'd seen him again...

No, it was better to cut things off quickly and get on with her life. She was going to Sara's baby shower. That was her goal right now. Anything else was just an obstacle in her path.

The lights of Las Vegas lit the sky for a long time before the city itself came into sight. She took the first exit for the Strip and cruised into the parking lot at the Camelot. It had been great of Jen to loan the car to her. She'd hesitated to take the younger woman into her confidence, but when she came right down to it, she had to trust someone once in a while or life was completely unbearable. And Jen had certainly come through for her. She had a cousin who lived in Las Vegas and would drive the car back. Hailey had given Jen some money for the cousin, and a gift of cash for Jen, as well, so she didn't feel particularly guilty about the whole arrangement. Everyone had come out ahead, the way she saw it.

Leaving the car locked, she hailed a cab and fidgeted for the whole ride into the downtown area. Once she exited the cab, she lost herself in the surging crowds that jammed the sidewalks of Glitter Gulch, finally stepping into the Bahamas Hotel and booking a room under an assumed name.

"Now, how can anyone find me?" she asked herself. They couldn't. It was impossible. She checked into her room, booked a flight to Denver for the first thing in the morning and took a little nap. Once she'd rested she would be able to think clearly again. Maybe.

How the hell was he going to find her? He found the car easily enough, so he knew she'd made it to Las Vegas, but just as he'd supposed, she hadn't registered at the Camelot. There was no way he could check every hotel, and even if he could, she wouldn't have taken a room under her real name. He knew Hailey and she was no dummy.

There was only one thing left to do. Going back to the airport, he found out when the next flight left for Denver. World Airway had one leaving at eight in the morning. He located the World Airway counter and hung around for a while, flirting with the pretty girl who worked there. One thing led to another and soon he got a look at the log of incoming reservation calls. Very conveniently, the times the calls were made were jotted down beside the notation of name and telephone contact number. It seemed a Ms. Candy Truesdale had called in just a half hour before, booking a seat on the Denver flight. He quickly copied down the telephone number she'd given and went to a copy of the yellow pages at the public phone bank. It didn't take long to match the number with the Bahamas Hotel, and to get the number for Ms. Truesdale from the clerk.

In the meantime, he put in a call to Donagan, just to let him know he hadn't fallen off the edge of the earth. When Donagan's answering machine picked up, Mitch was relieved. He didn't want to face Donagan's wrath at the moment. He had other things to do. But he left the Bahamas Hotel number and a cryptic message. "Don't worry. I've got something to take care of. I'll contact you as soon as I can." Then he made arrangements for the care of the airplane and left for downtown Las Vegas.

He tried calling her from the lobby, but there was no answer in her room, so he made his way up as though he knew what he was doing, and knocked on the door. Still no answer. Now what? He didn't want to take a chance on missing her. Somehow, he had to get into that room.

He stood in the hallway thinking for a moment, and as he thought, a maid came off the service elevator, her cart full of items for replenishing the rooms of the guests. An idea clicked in his brain right away.

"Ah," he said, smiling at the maid. "You're just the person I've been looking for. My wife needs some fresh towels."

The maid was young and pretty. It had been his experience that pretty young women seemed to respond to his smile, so he used it. And she smiled right back.

"Towels?" she asked. "Oh, certainly." Reaching into the bowels of her cart, she produced two thick, fluffy ones. "Here you are," she said, dimpling prettily.

"Thanks," he said, giving her a generous tip. "I appreciate it." Turning back toward the room, he pretended exasperation. "Oh no," he said to the maid. "Now look what

I've done." Another smile, this time one of self-deprecation. "I've locked myself out."

She laughed merrily. "Oh, everyone does that all the time. Here, let me help you." Bringing out a thick set of keys, she selected the one for the room he wanted to enter and stuck it in, opening the door for him. "There you go."

He saluted and gave her another smile. "Thank you," he said, waiting for her to start back down the hall before he went in. Sometimes all it took was just a little charm and a friendly smile.

He closed the door softly and looked around the room. The bed had been slept in and the shower was running in the bathroom. Turning, he stared at the bathroom door. The towels were still draped over his arm. It didn't take conscious effort to move him toward the door. He went as though compelled by some force beyond thought, beyond his control.

The bathroom was lined with mirrors, all of them fogged up by the steam her shower was emitting. She'd obviously been showering for some time. He stood watching her shadow as it moved behind the curtain, knowing he shouldn't be there but not caring a whole lot at the moment. Just knowing she was there seemed to fill him with something hot and urgent.

Somehow she sensed his presence. Maybe she saw him through the mist. Suddenly she went still and called out, "Who's there?"

"It's only me, ma'am," he replied. "The towel boy."

There was a moment of shocked silence, and then she called out incredulously, "The towel boy?"

"Yes, ma'am. You see, there was a steam alert from this bathroom, so they sent me up with fresh towels for you, just in case—"

"Mitch?" she shrieked, ripping open the shower curtain and leaning out. "Oh, my God," was all she could manage to say, once she'd come face-to-face with him. Her hand went to her mouth and she stared at him, water cascading over her, completely oblivious to anything but the sight of him in her bathroom. For a moment, she wasn't sure if she was dreaming or entirely awake. "Mitch?" she whispered again, just to make sure.

He didn't wait for her to come to her senses. What good would that do, anyway? Dropping the towels on the floor, he moved quickly, taking her head between his two large hands and kissing her soundly, covering her mouth with his own, filling himself with her sweet taste.

Was she crying? She wasn't sure. She felt as though she were crying and laughing at the same time, but she couldn't really tell, because the shower was still going and she was so wet. He was getting wet, too, his shirt sticking to his wide chest. She looked at him and held him and pushed away fear. He was here and, she realized suddenly, there was nothing she wanted more than to be with him.

He was just as bad. He'd spent days being careful, holding back. That was over now. It had taken all his moxie to find her, and now that he had her, he was going to show her...what? He didn't know. It didn't really matter.

He didn't have time to look at her. It was a time for feeling, and he felt her wet body, so slick and warm from the water. His hands slid down her, taking in the sensation of her firm flesh, so soft he could melt into her, so smooth he couldn't stay away—the dimpled spine, the nipped-in waist, the rounded hips—his hands came to rest cupping her bottom and pulling her closer to him. He wasn't going to be able to turn away this time, and he knew it. He wanted her desperately, as though his life depended on it. He had to have her. There was no longer any choice.

She was arching against him, her arms around his neck, her body an offering she made freely, and at the same time, she was making tiny animal sounds deep in her throat. She needed him as much as he needed her, needed him as she'd never needed another man. She wanted his possession, needed to feel his mastery in a way she wouldn't have admitted in saner moments. But she wanted it now, wanted his passion to sweep into her, carry her along with it, wipe every rational thought from her mind.

His mouth on hers was no longer gentle. They'd been holding back too long to take it easy now. He meant to devour her, one way or another, and she responded in kind, answering each thrust with her own, craving his hardness, matching his urgency. They were going a little wild, and she was glad of it.

Her life had been too full of withdrawals, of regrets and uncertainty. This she was sure of. This she would handle. This she would never regret.

He swept her up into his arms and carried her wet, naked body to the bed, laying her out on the golden spread, looking down at her beautiful form, running his hand over every part of her until he thought he would go mad with the tight, hot need he felt, the need that was thickening his blood and filling his brain with a sound like a buzz saw screaming.

He lowered his head, taking her nipple into his mouth and beginning a tantalizing rhythm of seduction with his tongue. She cried out, wrapping her legs around him, letting her body give him an involuntary invitation to join her in the dance as ancient as the seas. He drew away, his breath ragged in his throat, and began to shed his wet clothes. She lay back watching him, catching her breath, still moving in a mist of heat and desire, seeing red and white in waves, glorying in the beauty of his body as he revealed it, reaching out to touch him, to slide her hand along his hard flesh and gasp at the strength of him.

Writhing, he groaned, then drew back. "Wait," he said, fumbling in his pocket for protection and she had a blind, irrational urge to knock it out of his hand. She wanted him. He was all the protection she needed. She wanted him, and in some ways, she even wanted his baby. But she knew that was crazy, and she rejected it the moment the thought entered her head. She couldn't just blithely have a baby without preparing for it, making sure it would have a father and a stable home. Anything else was selfish, purely selfish.

But as she lifted her hips and took him in, she cradled his soul, as well as his body, and as the waves of sensation tore into her, leaving her gasping and breathless, her eyes opened wide with surprise at how it felt, how it really felt, when the right man was a part of it all.

He felt the release, felt it burst from him like the explosion of the sun, and he groaned, catching his breath as it faded, and then he sank his head into the hollow of her neck, kissing her softly, letting his tongue make moist trails across her skin and murmuring something she couldn't understand.

It was over. She lay back, stunned. She'd never known it could be like this. Suddenly all the love songs, all the romantic stories, began to make sense in her brain. So this was what it was like. And then came the hard question, right on the heels of that discovery. Was she in love? Was she really?

"Oh," she breathed, giving voice to her delight. Turning, she stretched and pressed herself against him, wanting as much flesh contact as she could get. "Let's do that again."

He laughed low in his throat and nibbled at her ear. "We can't do that again," he told her softly.

She raised her head and frowned at him. "What do you mean?"

He smiled and ran his hand through her thick, wild hair. "That was our first time," he told her. "We can never have that again."

She thought for a moment, then smiled. "Okay," she said. "Shall we keep track? From now on, every time we make love, it will be the only time we do it." She reached out, taking him in her hand. "This will be the second time," she told him serenely. "Pay attention because we'll never have a second time again."

"Not yet," he protested. "I'm not built like you. You've got to give me a couple of minutes."

But it turned out he was wrong. With a quick pause to turn off the shower before they were swept away in a flood, it only took seconds, and they were rolling again, joining together as wildly as they had the first time, making it last even longer, and coming away from it even more out of breath.

"Wow," Mitch admitted between gasps. "If it's just going to get more and more intense, I may have to take out a new insurance policy. I'm not sure I'm going to last."

"Don't worry," she told him, laughing. "I'll take good care of you."

Almost an hour went by before they came down to earth, with Mitch muttering about how he was going to go and finish the shower he'd started to join her in, and Hailey poking him with her big toe. Wrapped in a sheet, she sat back against the headboard and frowned as she contemplated his long, muscular body. Her hair, still damp, clung to her neck and shoulders, but she didn't notice. She was busy worrying.

His being here complicated everything. Her being half in love with him made it even worse. She'd planned to escape all the hassles and spend a nice weekend in Denver helping Sara prepare for her baby shower. Now what was she going to do?

"Oh, Mitch, why did you come?" she wailed, shaking her head.

He looked up and wished she hadn't brought it up. He was going to have to ask himself the same question, but not now. He wasn't yet ready to fabricate a satisfactory answer. She was too close and that tended to cloud his logical thinking. Instead of answering, he shrugged and countered with, "Tell me why you ran."

She thought for a moment and reached for him casually. "Because I can't trust anyone right now."

His eyes were luminous, watchful. "Even me?"

She smiled, outlining his lips with her finger. "Even you."

"Then why...?" He gestured toward the rumpled bed.

She laughed, the sound a light rumble that had its source deep in her soul. "Because you're just so irresistible," she told him. "But you knew that, didn't you?"

He rolled on his back, taking her with him. "Does that mean you're going to run away from me again?" he asked her as his arms tightened around her.

She shook her head slowly. "I don't think so," she whispered, curling her fingers into his dark hair. She couldn't promise, though, could she?

And he didn't ask her to. He knew she couldn't trust him. She'd said so. And why should she trust him? He'd been lying to her from the beginning. And when she found out...

"Why can't you trust your father?" he asked her suddenly, and she reared back, startled.

"Who said I couldn't trust my father?" she demanded, shifting away from him.

"You did. With every look, everything you've done."

She wanted to fight him on it, but suddenly her shoulders sagged. "I love my father," she said slowly, looking away from Mitch's blue eyes. "I...we lost my mother when I was young, and since then, we've only had each other."

He waited, but she didn't go on. "That sounds like a situation made for trust," he said softly. "What happened?"

She looked at him, and suddenly she drew farther away, curling into a ball, holding her knees with her arms, her eyes remote.

"What happened, Hailey?" he said, frowning and beginning to worry. "He didn't...hurt you?"

Her green gaze flashed down on him. "Oh, no. Nothing like that," she reassured him quickly. "He just...lied." She looked away again. "I know that doesn't sound like much, but believe me, it can be. I never knew for sure how we stood, whether I could count on him. He'd tell me one thing and then I would find out it was really not like that. He had this need to appear better all the time—even to me, his daughter." She shrugged. "It's not so bad any longer. I just take everything he says with a grain of salt and don't count on him too much. That was why I was so unsure about this whole trial business, about what was actually going on." She looked at Mitch's serious face and laughed. "Hey, it's no big deal. He's been very good to me. And like I say, I love him." She dismissed all that with a wave of her hand. "Take your shower so we can go eat dinner. I'm famished."

He rose obediently, and when he paused to kiss her, she let her tongue flicker out and surprise him. He deepened the kiss, then drew back. "And this from the lady who swore she was platonic forever," he said in a teasing tone. "Nice to see you're not stuck in your ways."

She laughed and watched him go on to the bathroom, but something he'd said bothered her and she frowned, trying to figure out what it was. Wait a minute—that "platonic" quote. When had she said that to him? Wasn't it...?

Before she'd nailed it down, the telephone rang and she looked at it in surprise. She hadn't told anyone she was here. Maybe Mitch had. The shower was already running, so she picked up the receiver.

"Hello?"

The voice on the other end sounded angry and said, without preamble, "Let me talk to Harper."

Harper? Oh, he meant Mitch. "Sorry, he's in the shower right now. May I tell him who called?"

The man gave a grunt of pure disgust. "Yeah, you can tell him Donagan called. I got his message on my answering machine. You tell him, what the hell does he think he's doing taking my plane off to Las Vegas to shack up with some bimbo." He coughed. "Uh, excuse me, ma'am, but I'm mad. Nothing personal. You just tell him I'm not running an R and R service here. I pulled a good man off the Palm Springs investigation to replace him so he could get off that ranch and get into something of more substance than spying on rich girls, like he's been demanding for days now, and so where the hell is he? I need him, and I need him now." He swore, then went on. "You tell him the D.A. asked me where the hell he was. Asked for him by name. And I couldn't tell him. Just tell him that."

Slightly stunned, she said automatically, "Do you want me to have him call you back?"

"No, I do not want any call back. I want my plane back,
and I want him back by morning or he's fired. You just tell
him that."

"I'll . . . I'll tell him."

"Thanks." He was calming down and obviously regretting a few of the things he'd said. "Uh . . . you a friend of
his?" he said.

"No," she replied simply. "I'm just a bimbo. Don't you
worry about me."

And she slammed down the telephone, then turned slowly
to stare at the bathroom door. Mitch was singing. She could
hear him from where she sat. Donagan's words were still
whirling in her head and she had yet to make heads or tails
of them. "Investigation . . . spying on rich girls . . . the D.A."

Rising from the bed, she dressed quickly. She heard the
water go off, and then he was whistling. When he came out,
a towel wrapped tightly around his slim hips, drops of water still sparkling in his eyelashes, he found her sitting on the
edge of the bed and staring out with blank eyes.

"Hey," he said, stopping and looking down at her.
"What's the matter?"

She turned her gaze up slowly until it met his. Looking at
him, she realized she'd been crazy to ever think of him as a
ranch hand. He had an urban look about him that was un-
mistakable. How could she have been so stupid?

"You had a phone call," she said dully.

His body went very still and his eyes seemed to light with
an unearthly glow. "Who?" he asked.

"Some man named Donagan."

Swearing, he dropped down to sit beside her. "I knew I
shouldn't have left this number with him," he muttered,
cursing himself.

"He wants his airplane back," she said. "And he says if
you don't get to work on the Palm Springs investigation by
morning, you're fired. Oh, and the D.A. has been asking
where you are."

He glanced at her sideways and shook his head. "Hailey..." he began tentatively, but then he didn't know what to say.

"So there were Artie and Bill watching me," she said slowly. "And then there were the mob guys. And the local cops. And you." She turned and looked into his eyes, her own wide and startlingly green. "You're just another one of them, aren't you? You've been watching me from the beginning."

"Hailey..." He tried to take her in his arms, but she pulled away, not letting him touch her.

"Will you please get dressed?" she asked him roughly, holding back her emotions as best she could. Something had broken open deep inside her and the pain was spilling out. The only way she was going to be able to keep things together was to express her anger. If she didn't do that, she would fall apart. "I can't yell at a naked man. Somehow it just doesn't work. And I really want to yell at you in the worst way."

He hesitated, then reached for his jeans. "Okay, but let me explain," he said as he pulled them on.

But she wasn't listening. She didn't want explanations. She just wanted to vent her rage, her frustration. "Is there anyone left who isn't watching me?" she demanded, pacing while he dressed. "Lord, how I wish I could find someplace where no one cares who I am."

"There are reasons, Hailey," he told her, pulling on his shirt. "Listen, at least I'm one of the good guys. There are plenty of bad ones out there looking for you."

"Too bad. They'll never find me now."

"Oh, yeah? If I figured it out, they can figure it out."

She tossed back her hair. "I'll deal with that when I have to. Right now I only have to deal with you."

He tried to approach her again. "Hailey, listen. You've got to be protected."

"Yes. I'd like to be protected." Her face contorted for a moment and she grabbed a pillow and threw it at him as hard as she could. "From you!" she yelled.

He took the pillow full in the face and didn't duck, because he knew he deserved it. "It's my job," he began, trying to explain as he slipped into his boots.

"Your job! Your job to lie and cheat and make people think you—" her face crumpled "—you feel things you don't really feel."

Mitch swung around and grabbed her, forcing her to stay in his arms, holding her tightly and smoothing her hair.

"Hailey, listen to me. What we did here today—"

"Oh God." Jerking away from him, she covered her face with her hands and he stood helplessly close but not touching her.

"What we did here today," he told her gently, "had nothing to do with...with me watching you. I swear to God. It was just you and me, man and woman, and it had nothing to do with who we are."

"Really?" Raising her head, she searched his eyes. "But how will I ever know the truth?" she asked wonderingly, her eyes misting slightly as she looked at him.

Her misery was like a knife in his heart, but he didn't know how to tell her, how to make her understand. Their situation was something he didn't even understand himself, so how could he comfort her? He shook his head, reaching for her. "I'm not going to lie to you, Hailey," he began.

Her head rose quickly. "Oh, that's a good one," she interrupted with a mocking laugh as she pulled away from him again. "Ha-ha. Very funny, cowboy."

He followed her across the room, not wanting to let her go, wanting to make her see, somehow, that what happened when they first met, first knew each other, had nothing to do with now. "I mean it. I had to lie to..."

Swinging around, she glared at him accusingly. "You lied to me at the dance club, didn't you?"

He took a deep breath. "Yes."

Her eyes narrowed. "You knew from the beginning who I was."

He nodded.

She closed her eyes and shook her head. "And you let me go on, acting like a fool."

"You didn't act like a fool. Hailey, you're a class act from beginning to end."

Opening her eyes, she stared at him, trying not to cry. "And this is the end, cowboy," she said, her voice shaking. She made a jerking motion toward the door with her thumb. "You're out of here."

"Hailey..." He tried to move toward her, but she stepped back and avoided him.

"Go," she ordered, pointing toward the door. "Go, or I'll call security."

He hesitated. The last thing he wanted to do was to leave her. But he could see it was no use right now. She was hurt and she wanted to hurt back. She wouldn't let him stay. It might be better to leave her alone, let her get over it as best she could. If she could. And besides, he had a few things to think over himself.

When he finally faced that reality, he left, but only to the lobby where he kept watch on who came and went all night long. He wasn't going to let one of the mob characters get to her now.

The night seemed to last forever, but he had a lot to think about. The first thing he had to do was figure out the answer to her question—why was he here? It wasn't like him to get more involved with a subject than he was with the outcome of the project. Why was Hailey different? The answer to that question was important to him—and at the same time, it scared him right down to his core.

He paced, he sat, and then he paced again, trying to think it out. Okay, so what was it? She was beautiful. She was attractive. She was warm and sexy and intriguing. But was that it? Was that what had drawn him here?

No, he reassured himself quickly. That wasn't it at all. She'd been in trouble, in danger, and he'd come to protect her. That was much closer to the mark. After all, he had a long history of coming to the rescue of anyone or anything that seemed to be in jeopardy. He'd started out when he was a kid, bailing out his own family when his father had hit the skids and become incapable of taking care of them. And ever since, it seemed he was always extricating someone from some precarious position they'd gotten themselves into. It was those very impulses that had brought him into law enforcement. He just couldn't help it.

Sure, he told himself as he headed to the coffee shop for a morning jolt of caffeine to prop his eyes open. Sure, that was all it was. Things had gone a little further than he'd planned, but that was over now. He was here to help her. When she no longer needed his help, he would be gone. It was that simple.

He caught sight of himself in the mirror along the side of the coffee shop and he stopped, stunned. He looked like hell. Oh, well. That was just another of the sacrifices he was prepared to put up with as long as it helped keep Hailey out of trouble. With a sigh, he went on in to the counter and ordered coffee.

He left for the airport half an hour later, before she showed up. Once there, he arranged to have a courier fly Donagan's plane back to Palm Springs and bought himself a ticket on the plane to Denver. Then he settled down behind a large newspaper to await her arrival. Now if he could just keep from falling asleep and missing the plane.

Ten

Hailey was running late and she didn't have time for coffee. When she arrived at the airport, she left her purse in the cab and had to chase him down the street to get it back. Then the metal detector kept going off and she had to shed two layers of clothing and all her rings before the silly malfunctioning mechanism would let her pass. She went to the wrong gate and almost boarded a plane to Minnesota. And finally, she was on the flight to Denver, sinking into her window seat with a sigh and leaning back, closing her eyes and trying to relax.

But it was hard to do that when her mind wouldn't be still. It had been racing all night, racing ever since she'd realized Mitch was not just some gorgeous and seductive cowboy who was somehow different from all the other men who had disappointed her all her life. No. Oh, no. Mitch was an investigator for the D.A.'s office, and his only real interest in her was purely professional in nature.

"Damn him!" she muttered, and not for the first time.

She should have known better. She'd thought she'd
learned. It never worked out with men. She was beautiful.
So what? Why did that seem to throw men for a loop? She'd
started young being the victim of her own beauty. At thir-
teen, the TV repairman had tried to sweet-talk her. At
fourteen, college boys were hanging around. By the time
she'd finished high school, every boy on the football team
and half of the Scholars Club had made passes, each more
insulting than the last.

Because they didn't really like me, she reminded herself
silently. They liked to be seen with her. They liked to score
points. Then each and every one of them went back to his
real girlfriend, all puffed up and proud that he thought he'd
gotten somewhere with the prettiest girl in school.

But when you came right down to it, this case was a little
different. She'd thought it was the same old thing at first.
But he hadn't acted the way most men did. The usual ea-
gerness had been missing. He'd seemed to accept her as a
human being, a woman. She'd been drawn to him. She'd
thought maybe, maybe this time it would be different.

Well, it was different, all right. This time, he was just
getting close to her so he could weasel things out of her. This
time, he didn't even care how she looked.

"Well, that's refreshing at least," she whispered, trying
to console herself. But it didn't really work. He was still a
jerk, and she was better off without him.

Still she couldn't help wondering where he was right now.
Probably in the plane he'd come in, winging his way to Palm
Springs, hoping not to get fired. Well, she was glad. At least
she didn't have to deal with him any longer.

Someone sat down in the seat beside her but she didn't
look up. She didn't want to get involved in any conversa-
tions today. She had too much on her mind. Maybe, if she
pretended to be asleep...

"Are you okay?" her seatmate asked, and her eyes shot
open.

Slowly she turned to face Mitch, who was sitting beside
her, strapping himself in with the seat belt as though it were

the most ordinary thing in the world that they should be seated side by side. The shock left her speechless for a moment, and when she spoke, her voice was raw.

"What do you think you're doing?" she demanded, eyes wide with amazement.

He gave her a pleasant look and settled back. "Going to Denver. Just like you."

"No." She shook her head, hardly able to digest this bit of news. "No, you can't."

"But I can," he told her simply. "And I am."

She was still shaking her head. "What are you doing this for?" she demanded.

"I'm watching over you," he said, facing her and thinking she looked awfully good this morning.

She mouthed the words *Watching over me?* then said aloud, "Can't you do it from somewhere a little farther away?" She was beginning to feel real anger. "Like maybe from Chicago?"

"Sorry," he told her, reaching for the magazines stuck in the seat in front of him. "Anything good to read in these?"

She was fuming, burning up, and trying desperately to think of a way to get him to go. "You might as well know right now," she said evenly. "If you stay, I'm not talking to you."

He glanced up and smiled at her. "That's okay. We don't have to talk."

She threw her hands up, palms out, bewildered. "You don't even want to talk? Then go away."

He shook his head. "No, I can't." His gaze grew more serious. "Because I have to make sure you're okay," he said softly.

She could see he was earnest, but that didn't matter to her at the moment. She wanted him gone, out of sight. Seeing him like this just rubbed salt in the wounds. The sooner she could get rid of him, the sooner she could start forgetting about him. And that was her main goal right now.

"Hey," she told him forcefully. "I'm okay. Look at me. I'm fine. Now will you go away?"

He looked at her and winced. She was so beautiful. "That's not good enough," he told her, regret in his voice.

She was going to go crazy. She felt like tearing out her hair. "What do you need, a signed affidavit? A sample of my blood?" She grabbed a strand of hair and shook it at him. "How about a lock of my hair? Would that do?"

"Calm down," he told her quietly. "I won't go away, no matter what kind of scene you make. So you might as well relax."

She wanted to scream, but she forced herself to remain calm and tried another tact. "Mitch, you have to go. Please. Go now."

"No, I can't." He frowned at her, shifting so that he could face her fully. "Listen, this is the way it is. You're in danger from the mob. There has been plenty of evidence of that. I'm going to stay with you until we're sure you're out of danger. It's as simple as that."

She stared at him. He was serious. He really thought he could tag along for the rest of her life if he felt like it.

"No," she said firmly, shaking a finger under his nose. "It's as simple as this. I don't want you watching me. I can take care of myself. I want you gone." She turned her head.

"Oh, miss!" She called to the stewardess and beckoned for her. "This man is bothering me," she said pleasantly to the round-faced woman who glanced at Mitch with a knowing eye. "Could you please move him to another seat, somewhere very far away?"

The flight attendant looked from Hailey to Mitch and back again, hesitating. Then she leaned close to Mitch's ear and whispered, "Is this the one you told me about?"

He nodded and touched her arm. "Don't worry," he told her while Hailey looked on, gaping in amazed horror. "I've got things under control. She won't be a problem."

"Okay." The woman smiled at him with pure sympathy. "I really admire what you're doing here. She's lucky to have you."

"Thanks," he said with a smug smile as she turned and went to another passenger.

Hailey glared at him and punched him in the arm. "What was that all about?" she demanded through gritted teeth.

He sighed, rubbing the spot where her punch had landed. "I didn't want to have to tell you, but I told the crew and the attendants that you were emotionally disturbed and I was taking you home for treatment. I warned them you might try to get rid of me." He smiled at her. "They were very cooperative."

"Oh!" She clenched her fists. "Why would she believe such a thing?"

"I guess I look trustworthy to them. And anyway, I showed her my badge."

She felt as though she were about to explode. "You...!"

He grinned at her, taking her hands in his and leaning toward her. "Watch your language. We've got rules to cover people like you."

She couldn't do anything but glare at him. "I hate you, you know."

He shrugged. "That's okay. That's good, actually."

"Good?" She yanked her hands away. "Why is it good?"

He looked earnest again, the solid citizen. "Because it would be best to keep things platonic between us."

She stared at him, then folded her arms across her chest and pouted. "That was my idea from the beginning," she muttered.

"I know. I give you all the credit for it. You were right. I was wrong."

She sighed, the fight dying in her. What could she do? The plane was taking off and he was obviously here for the entire ride. "Well, at least you know superiority when you come up against it," she said sulkily.

"Oh yes," he murmured. "That I do." Suddenly his hand was encasing hers, his fingers lacing with hers, and he leaned close. "Hailey. I'm sorry."

She stared at their hands for a moment, then raised her face until she met his gaze. "What are you sorry for?" she asked softly, looking into his blue eyes.

"That I had to lie to you. That I...that we...that things happened before I'd told you the truth about who I am."

She searched his eyes, looking for something she wasn't finding. "Do you feel like a rat?" she asked him.

He blinked but didn't back off. "Yes, I guess I do."

"Good." She almost smiled. "Do you wish you were dead?" she added.

His wide mouth twisted at the corners. "No. Actually, I don't."

She frowned. "Then we haven't hit the depths of your guilt yet. Keep going."

His hand tightened on hers. "Sorry, but I've gone about as far as I can."

She gazed at him speculatively, her mouth turned down at one corner. "So the rat thing is as far as you'll go?"

He nodded, his eyes sparkling. "Just about."

Her chin rose and her eyes narrowed. "Then I don't forgive you."

He met her gaze and looked at her seriously. "I don't care if you forgive me. I just want to make sure you make it through the day, Hailey. That's all that matters to me right now."

He meant it. He really meant it. She could see it in his eyes. Suddenly she was ashamed of herself. She was acting like that old spoiled brat again and she knew it. Slowly, firmly, she disentangled their fingers and drew away from him.

"Okay," she told him evenly. "You can be my bodyguard for now. But no touching. Got that?"

"Got it." He looked at her for a moment, then sat back and stared straight in front of him. She was right. No touching. It was much better that way. If only she wasn't so damned tempting, things would be easier. But nobody said it had to be easy. They only said it had to be done right. And that was how he meant to do it.

The trip to Denver was quiet with each of them deep in thought. They had a short argument in the Denver airport about whether or not she still needed guarding, but Mitch

won, saying he wanted to check out where she was staying
before leaving her, and they shared a cab to her condo. On
his suggestion, they changed cabs halfway there, just in case,
to throw off anyone who might be trying to trace her steps
later on.

"They would never find me here," she insisted as they got
out and started up the long walk lined with pines to the
glass-and-redwood condo. "My father put this place in my
name. I doubt if they'll be expecting that."

"Oh, it's yours?"

"Not exactly." She grimaced. "In fact, I've never been
here before. But he's been putting a lot of things in my name
lately. There's a beach house in San Diego and a cabin in
Washington state. I don't really know why he's doing it.
Something for financial reasons, he told me."

Salting away properties for when he turned state's evidence, Mitch thought to himself, but he didn't say a word
to her about it. "So they're not really yours."

She shook her head, extracting a key, trying to hurry, as
a cold rain was beginning to fall. "No. Paperwork only. But
I can use any of them anytime I want, and he had keys made
for me."

She turned the key in the lock and opened the door. Mo-
tioning her aside, Mitch went in before her and systemati-
cally went through the place, checking closets and showers,
before turning back and nodding. "It seems to be okay," he
said.

"Yes." She didn't say *I told you so,* because she wasn't
feeling very cocky right now. He would be leaving soon.
And suddenly that seemed a great tragedy.

"You sure you're going to be okay here all by yourself?"
he asked, turning slowly to look at the place. It was lavishly
furnished with a huge crystal chandelier hanging in the entryway and an open staircase leading up to a loft. This was
a proper setting for her, a setting unlike anything he would
ever live in. He ought to go, he ought to get out of here and
leave her alone. She was right. There really wasn't much
chance anyone would find her now. The danger had been at

the airport, and on the plane. The last hazard had been if someone had already arrived and was waiting for her, but that hadn't happened, either. She was going to be all right. He should stop worrying and get back to his own life.

"I'll be fine," she told him. "You'd better get going. I heard someone say there's a storm coming. You'll want to get out ahead of it."

"You're right." He shoved his hands into his pockets and looked at her, not moving toward the door.

"Will you be able to get your job back?" she asked him.

He shrugged. He hadn't given the matter much thought. "I don't know. It will depend on how mad Donagan is."

She hesitated. "Do you want me to...?"

"No." He took her hand in his and smiled down at her. "No, I don't want you to do anything. You just...have a happy life. Okay?"

She stared up at him. "You, too."

He lost himself in her gaze for what seemed like centuries, and then, finally, it was time to go. He dropped her hand and turned toward the door, taking the steps as though he were going toward his doom. As he reached it, he turned back, his hand on the knob and looked at her.

"I don't feel right about this," he said softly.

She came to him quickly. "I know," she agreed nervously. "It feels...almost as though there's something else we should do before you go."

He nodded slowly and, taking his hand off the knob, turned toward her. "I think I know what it is," he said, his eyes dark and deep in the shadows.

She stared up into his eyes. "What?"

He bent toward her, his hand in her hair. "I think...I think maybe we should make love one more time," he said softly.

She didn't flinch. Instead she looked steadily at him and didn't say a word.

He raised one eyebrow. "Do you want to?" he asked.

She swayed toward him, nodding, her eyes barely brimming with a smile. "I want to," she whispered.

He didn't ask her again. Tilting her face toward his, he kissed her lips, first gently, then hungrily. "Where's the bedroom?" he asked, his voice low and husky.

How was she supposed to know, she thought, somewhat hysterically. He'd explored the place more than she had. But she led the way to the bedroom she'd noticed at the back of the ground floor, led the way to the opulent bed that took up half the room and opened out like an offering to a sun god.

"I guess this is it," she murmured, looking around while he nibbled on her neck and let his hands slide slowly down her sides and then back up to capture her breasts. She pulled away, looking up at him nervously. She knew she shouldn't be doing this. It went against all her resolutions. But he was so...so...

"Now...now don't take this personally," she said as he went on kissing her, his arms winding around her, his body making its own bid at seduction. "You've got to understand. This doesn't mean I've changed my mind about anything."

Lifting her, he carried her to the huge bed and dropped her onto it, but she went on talking. "Really, I'm not going to expect anything from you. It's...I just want to prove to myself that last night wasn't a dream. That I can feel that way again. That..."

His hands framed her face and he looked down at her lips, his eyes as blue as Asian seas. "Will you please shut up?" he growled, then covered her mouth with his own and showed her how to communicate without words.

She strained toward him, all inhibitions and doubts falling away like leaves off an autumn tree. It was so good with him, so natural and right. No other man had ever made her feel so light, so free, like flying.

His hands were quick and effective, sliding her clothes off her before she realized what he was doing. She felt the cool air on her naked skin and writhed, twisting to follow when his hot mouth left her breast, reaching to tug on his clothes, wanting to feel skin to skin, soul to soul, wanting all of him, quickly and very, very deep.

But he wasn't in a hurry this time, and he made her wait. His long fingers stroked the sensitive valley between her shoulder blades and down to nestle up against her tailbone. She moaned and turned, pulling his head back down so she could capture his mouth with her own, gasping when his leg came between hers and sent a shudder through her.

"Mitch," she whispered, her entire body quivering with a wave of desire that stunned her. "If you make me wait any longer, I'll leave you behind."

He laughed low in his throat, and then reared back to survey her, feeling primitive, as though he'd conquered something, when he knew it was much closer to a conquest for her than for him. Still, for the moment, she was his. And he felt it, felt it in his loins, felt it in his heart. And then he was ready.

They came together like two wild things, reaching and gasping and clutching each other, thrusting harder and higher and making greedy demands that shamed neither of them. Her body came alive, throbbing with a vitality she hadn't known she was capable of, creating a heat that swept over them both like a wave, carrying them higher and higher, until it crested, and they were tumbling back down into the covers like creatures whose wings had slowly folded.

She lay back and wanted to purr, like a big, old, contented cat. His arms were still wrapped around her, his head in the hollow of her shoulder. She'd never felt so loved and so loving, so at peace and so excited. She knew something now, knew it clearly. She was in love with this man, this cowboy, this lying sneak who wanted only to protect her. She didn't want him to leave.

So when she realized he was asleep in her arms, she didn't rouse him. Carefully she reached down to pull the covers over the two of them, and she let herself drift off, as well.

It was hours later when they woke. The wind was whistling past the eaves and when Hailey looked out, she found a blizzard encasing their world and leaving them as isolated as though they had paddled out to a desert island and lost the oars.

Slipping back into bed, she cuddled close to him. He kissed her, then craned his neck to see the clock.

"Good Lord, I've got to get going," he muttered, stretching and yawning very widely.

"Oh yeah?" she said, cuddling closer. "Think again, Mr. Genius."

He looked down at her and smiled at the teasing light in her eyes. "What's the matter?" he asked.

"You're not going anywhere," she told him smugly. "There's a storm raging outside. We're snowed in."

He went stiff with shock. "You're kidding," he said, then jumped out of bed and went to the window to see for himself. "Oh, my God."

A vision of Donagan's face ran through his mind, but it faded fast, and he turned slowly and looked at the woman waiting for him in the bed. He didn't have to leave her yet, and a feeling of joy came over him such as he'd never experienced before. It shook him. He didn't know quite how to handle it. A part of him wanted to run, wanted to get away from someone who could have such a powerful effect on him. But the rest of him wanted to get back in that bed and hold her close. And that is what he did.

They made love again, slow and easy this time, each of them almost lethargic, hands trailing lightly over sensitive body parts, hips moving together in a slow, erotic waltz, and then they climbed to a peak even higher than anything they'd managed before, and Hailey closed her eyes very tightly and declared that she loved him, but only in her head. She didn't dare say it aloud. She didn't want to scare him away. Not just yet.

And he was scared. She had him trapped and he felt like a tiger in a cage. He didn't know which way to turn or what to do to get free of this bond that was growing between them, strengthening every moment, thickening and tightening, binding him to her. It couldn't be. He wasn't in the market for "forever" sorts of vows. Surely she knew that.

When the time came, he was going to leave her. Surely she knew that, too. But then, why was it hurting him so much to think about it? That didn't make any kind of sense that he could think of.

They put on robes and made a fire and pattered around the kitchen, digging up old canned and boxed food and making a strange stew that they gulped down like ravenous beasts. They didn't pay any more attention to what time it was, or even what day it was. They slept when they felt like it, ate when the mood hit them, made love more than any pair should be allowed to. And other than that, they lay in each other's arms and talked and stroked each other and got closer and closer all the time.

He'd never known a woman before who could get so much of his background out of him. Before he knew it, he was telling her about his father, something he'd never told anyone.

She couldn't believe she'd finally met a man who listened—really listened! And then reacted thoughtfully to what she'd said instead of laughing it off as something cute or silly.

And they found they had so much in common. They both loved old Cary Grant movies and margaritas with lime and roller coasters and grated cheese on their pizza. And the more she talked to him the more she was convinced that, despite the fact that he'd lied to her, he was the most honest man she'd ever met. He had a basic integrity that made her think of a conversation they'd had at the dance club that first night. She'd tossed her coin into the fountain and wished for an honest man, and he'd asked her how she would know if he were honest or not.

As she remembered, she'd said, "I think I would be able to tell. There would be something about him...something..."

"Something honest," he'd offered.

And she'd laughed. "Right. Exactly."

And that was precisely how it was.

All was not perfect, however. They talked of many things, but they never talked about the future. Neither one of them wanted to think about what was going to happen when the snow melted. Because neither one of them knew.

But reality had to intrude at some point. It was late afternoon of the second day when it finally did. They were making love in the den, just for variety's sake. They'd been playing, teasing each other. They'd gone outside in the snow and when they came in, Mitch brought a handful of the icy stuff to put down Hailey's back, making her scream and go after him with the chunks she could save. They ended up in the den, wrestled, and quickly turned the mock fight into real lovemaking, yanking at each other's clothes and panting, half-laughing, and coming together with sharp cries, like a pair of young wolves.

Spent at last, they lay back, giggling like teenagers, and when they finally began to pull themselves together, Hailey noticed that their wild fun had knocked open a cabinet and papers were spilling out onto the floor.

Mitch was back into his clothes first and he bent down to begin picking up the mess. As he pulled the papers together, he glanced down at a bankbook that had fallen beneath them. A bankbook for a Swiss bank account.

It was as though everything inside him froze. He kept moving, kept picking up paper, and even noticed a letter addressed in handwriting to "Hailey, my sweet girl." But it was as though his mind were outside of his body, watching all this from the corner of the room. He walked, he talked, but he wasn't really there.

"There's a letter for you here," he said, stacking the papers and glancing through them quickly. "Maybe you'd better read it."

"A letter?" She came over and looked at it curiously, taking it from him. "That's my father's handwriting," she murmured as she tore it open.

She read quickly, and while she read, he surreptitiously flipped open the bankbook, noted the total, closed it again and slipped it into his pocket. Then he turned back to look at her.

Her face was ashen and her hands were trembling. But for some reason, he couldn't feel anything.

Her green eyes rose to meet his, wide and tragic. "Mitch," she said hoarsely. "You'd better look at this."

He didn't want to. For a moment, he contemplated telling her to put it away, to forget all about it. But he knew he couldn't do that. He couldn't forget about any of this. It was all part of his job, part of his responsibility.

Silently he held out his hand and took it from her. He quickly skimmed it, but there were no surprises as far as he was concerned. Her father loved her. He wanted to take care of her, and once he'd finished testifying, he was going into the witness protection program and he would be unable to see her for a long, long time. But he'd made provisions, set up properties, and put money in a bank account in Switzerland. He was sorry—sorry he couldn't tell her in person, sorry he hadn't told her the truth. She was to put the papers in the accompanying folder in a safe-deposit box and hide the key. Then she was to stay in Denver for a year before flying to Switzerland and taking charge of the money. When he felt it was safe, he would contact her. And once again, he loved her.

Mitch turned slowly and looked at Hailey. "You didn't have to show this to me," he told her, and half of him wished she hadn't.

She looked surprised. She'd calmed down, found her sea legs once again. She shook her head. "This was what you've been after all this time, isn't it?" she said, gesturing toward the papers. "Take them. It's your job."

He glanced at the papers. They seemed to be exactly what he'd been told to look for, incriminating evidence on a lot of people who were going to be very unhappy. But the money. The money was something else. Her father had probably made most of it illegally. It was his job to take it in until that could be determined. But Hailey...

"For once, my father doesn't get his way," she murmured, looking sad but in control.

"Hailey, your father was trying to guarantee your future," he told her quickly. "He thinks he's proving how much he loves you." It was touching, actually. The old man thought he could give his daughter all this money and make up for everything else he'd ruined by his actions. It wouldn't work, of course, but he was still trying.

"Don't hate him," he added, though he wasn't sure why he should be lobbying for the man. He jammed the papers into the folder and fingered the bankbook in his pocket. Had she seen it? She'd read about the money in her father's letter. Should he show her the book? He hadn't decided yet, wasn't sure what he was going to do. Because, when he came right down to it, he was just as anxious that Hailey's future be secure as her father was. There was a war going on inside him, a war between his duty and the way he felt about this woman. And right now, he wasn't sure which side was going to win.

She watched his face, fascinated, even though she was dying inside. What was he thinking? Did he despise her because of her father and what he'd done? Was he glad that they'd found the papers? Did that make it all worthwhile? Was he going to go back a hero now, because he'd found them, after all? And would he ever, ever think of her again?

Surely he would remember. Maybe on quiet evenings just before he went to sleep. They'd both known this was too good to last, and here was the end, coming full circle. They'd met because of these things, these papers, this evidence. Now they would separate because of them. After all, what kind of future was there for the two of them, even if he'd never had any thoughts along those lines? The law enforcement officer and the daughter of a man who was involved with the mob? Not a chance in hell, much less heaven. It was over.

She turned away, rubbing her arms as though she were cold, slightly overwhelmed by it all. These revelations about her father were part surprise, part recognition of some-

thing she'd always known but had been afraid to admit to.
She'd always known her father came too close to the line at
times, but she'd never dreamed he was actually so far into
the mob that he had enough information to interest the
government to this extent. More lies. But how could she
pretend to be surprised? This was her father. Always would
be.

So now, not only would she lose her father, but she would
lose her lover, as well. The man she loved, the men she
loved. All gone.

"Hailey." Mitch came up behind her. "Are you okay?"

She nodded and turned to give him a weak smile. "I'm
fine. Really. Don't worry about me, I'll be fine."

His hand touched her cheek, but she didn't look recep-
tive and he drew it back. "Hailey, I have to take the papers
back to the D.A.," he said, his eyes clouded with regret.

The papers. Yes, it had been the papers from the beginning. That, and the money. How much had it ever been her?

But she nodded, not blaming him in any way. "Hey,
there's nothing else a Dudley Do-Right like you would do. I
know that." And she smiled, because, despite her teasing
tone, she admired him for it. He really was the honest man
she'd been searching for all her life. And now she had
proven how unworthy of him she was.

He made a call to Donagan and told him he was coming
in. When he returned to the den, where Hailey was still
pacing the floor, he had news.

"The trial is over. The mobster was convicted and sen-
tenced to twenty years. Your father has gone into the program."

Her shoulders slumped. "So it's over," she said mus-
ingly, her eyes a deep, haunted moss green. "All over."

"Yes." Her sadness broke his heart, but there was something about the set of her spine that told him she didn't want
his sympathy, didn't want his touch right now. He turned
and went to take a shower.

He was ready to go in half an hour. The streets had been
plowed and cars were moving. All too soon the taxi was

honking outside. Mitch found Hailey and gave her a quick kiss on the lips. "What are you planning to do?" he asked her.

She shrugged, avoiding his gaze. "I'm going to Sara's baby shower. And after that, I suppose I'll start looking for a job. Denver seems like a nice place. I may just stay here."

He nodded. "Don't go back to California for a while," he advised. "Wait until they forget all about you."

She nodded. "I think I get the picture," she said, lifting her chin. "Don't worry about me, Mitch. I'm going to be fine."

"I know you are." He hesitated. "Thanks," he said awkwardly.

"Don't mention it," she replied crisply. "You'd better go."

He looked at her for much too long, then ducked his head and left the room. She didn't want to go to the door with him. Hugging her arms tightly, she turned and looked at the cabinet where they'd found the papers, then bent to pick up some scraps that had been left behind. Opening the cabinet door, she started to throw the scraps inside, but something caught her eye. She looked again. A little bankbook on a Swiss bank. She'd seen it in Mitch's hand, briefly, just before she read the letter from her father. It was the money he'd put aside for her. Why hadn't Mitch taken the bankbook? That was one of the main things he'd been looking for.

She stood stock-still. The answer was clear. He was pretending he hadn't seen it. He was leaving it behind for her.

"Oh, Mitch, no." Tears sprang to her eyes. She knew him now, and she knew this went against everything he stood for. He didn't lie and he did his duty. But he'd done this for her. And she couldn't let him.

Grabbing the book, she ran for the front door. He was already getting into the cab. Running down the walk, heedless of the cold, she reached the car just before he closed the door and tossed the bankbook in to him.

"I don't want it, Mitch," she told him quite seriously. "It's not mine. And I can't let you do this."

Holding the bankbook, he didn't say anything, but his gaze held hers as the cab backed out of the parking spot and turned toward the highway that led to the airport, and she kept watching until they drove out of sight. And then she went inside and cried.

The Baby Shower

Hailey was standing inside the huge plate glass window, watching a dark, handsome man scaling the outside of the house declare his love for her old roommate, Cami Bishop. The same Cami who'd sworn men were off her list. Hailey laughed with the others and applauded his declaration when they did, but inside her heart was in pain.

She was glad for Cami. *But what about me?* She couldn't help but think it.

She watched Sara with her new baby, watched her coo and laugh and then watched the man she called Drey lean down beside her and take the baby's hand, letting the little fingers curl around his big thumb, and a part of her shriveled inside.

She'd searched every shop in town for the perfect baby gift and had finally found a silver baby cup inscribed with the line, "Sweeten with love." She'd had it wrapped and delivered but she wished she could give the real thing. Real love—the ideal gift for anyone, not just for babies.

She was happy for Sara, but a part of her wanted so badly to have that, too. A baby. Her heart cried out for one.

Turning, she left the room and walked through the house. Where was J.J., anyway? J.J. was a career woman. She wouldn't be in love, not good old J.J. Once she got there, Hailey would feel she had someone who understood on her side.

"When is J.J. supposed to get here?" she asked when Sara found her looking at old pictures of the four roomies Sara kept on the wall of her den.

Sara looked distracted. "She should have been here by now."

"Have you heard from her?" Hailey asked.

"She called about an hour ago, said she was on her way." Sara frowned, remembering something. "Oh, she said to be watching for a bus." Looking at Hailey, she shook her head. "Isn't that strange? I don't know what she meant. We're not on any bus route way out here."

"A bus?" Hailey shook her head. "Why would she come on a bus?"

"I don't know. Oh, she said something about bringing in a busload of babies. That's J.J. Go figure." Throwing up her hands, Sara rushed off to take care of putting out the punch, and Hailey sighed. A busload of babies. What that meant, she had no idea, but it sounded so jolly, and she was still crying inside.

Everyone seemed so happy. Cami was in love. Sara had her baby. J.J. was involved in something exciting. And here was poor old Hailey, odd man out again.

"Self-pity will turn your hair green," she told herself sarcastically, gazing at her own reflection in the window-pane as the others swirled around her, laughing and drinking something purple Sara had called Barney punch. It seemed, once you had a baby, you entered a whole new world with its own vocabulary. It was a world Hailey didn't think she would ever get to visit.

It was silly, really. After all these years of thinking she would never marry, never find a man who would fit with her idiosyncrasies, never have a baby—she'd found Mitch. He'd been perfect in so many ways, and she loved him with an aching hunger that threatened to bring tears to her eyes at any given moment. Losing him had made a wreck of her. If someone said, "Hey, it looks like rain," she teared up. That very morning her neighbor at the condo had said, "Wasn't there a man with you when you first moved in?" and she'd sobbed like an infant for the next half hour. She was missing him, and she knew she would get over it someday, but right now, she was a mess.

If things had gone right, she might have had it all with that man. And that was what made it so infuriating. She'd been better off not knowing he existed, she decided. Better off not knowing what she was missing. Because now, she didn't know if her heart would ever mend.

"Okay, everybody," one of Sara's friends called out to the women. "We're going to play a game. I'll shout out a letter, and you write down every word starting with it that has anything to do with babies."

Hailey put down her hideous punch and melted back into the room. She made it a practice to avoid games at all costs, and this one sounded particularly tedious.

"Oh, watch out," a short, dark woman said to a redhead as they passed Hailey in the hall, both going eagerly toward the game she was avoiding. "You'll never get a chance like this again. Don't blow it."

Hailey stopped dead in her tracks. The woman wasn't talking to her. In fact, she had no idea what she was talking about. But the message seemed tailor-made for her. And suddenly it resonated deep inside.

You'll never get a chance like this again. Don't blow it.
Don't blow it.

A wave of near-nausea swept over her and it was as though a new window had opened on her world. She was in love. Right? So why wasn't she doing something about it?

Why wasn't she reaching for what she wanted? Sure, she didn't know how he felt about her. But how was she going to find out if she sat around here and moped about it? Not trying was like not breathing. It was giving up, and she had never been a quitter.

Mitch was in California. So what was she doing here? She paused, thinking quickly. California was supposed to be dangerous for her right now.

"So what?" she muttered. "Living without Mitch is what will kill me."

Yes, she would go.

"Sara!" She grabbed her friend around the waist and hugged her. "Your shower is lovely but I have to go. I just realized I'm in love! Really in love!"

Sara steadied her with a frown. "But...where are you going?"

"To the airport." Hailey shone with sudden radiance. "I have to go to him. I have to make him see..."

Her words trailed off because she was dashing for the door, grabbing her coat from the coatrack and heading for her car. "Goodbye," she called back. "Wish me luck!"

And all Sara could do was shake her head and turn back to her party.

Not fifteen minutes later, Mitch stood outside Sara's house and raked a hand through his thick black hair. He'd come all the way from Los Angeles and now he was hesitating. He felt like an idiot. Here he was, a veteran of undercover work with mobsters, an experienced agent who'd risked death a dozen times in his career, and he was nervous as hell about seeing Hailey again. In fact, his heart was racing as though he were about to walk into a dark alley where he knew he'd get shot at.

"I've done that before," he reminded himself. "I doubt if I'd get this nervous doing it again." He grimaced and turned apprehensively to look at his car. It appeared safe, and he was tempted to go back to it. "Bring on your gangsters,'' he muttered. ''Just save me from one medium-sized woman with spun gold hair and a smile that lights up the sky.''

What was he going to say to her? He didn't have a clue, wasn't even really sure why he'd come. Somehow, he'd had to. So here he was.

Gritting his teeth, he reached out and rang the bell. A tall woman with icy blond hair opened the door.

''Yes?'' she said.

''Uh. I'm looking for Hailey Kingston. Is she...?''

''Oh, my God.'' Sara covered her mouth with both hands as though to hold back a scream. ''I'll bet you're him, aren't you?''

Mitch looked behind himself, just to make sure. ''Who?'' he asked.

''Hailey's guy.'' Sara blanched. ''Oh, my God. Oh no.'' Turning inside, she grabbed a pretty woman with hair the color of ripe wheat. ''Cami, this is Hailey's guy. What'll we do with him?''

Cami took in the situation at a glance. She knew all about Hailey's hasty departure for the airport. But she also knew it might not be a good idea to tell him about it. She smiled at Mitch, who was looking more and more sorry that he'd come.

''We ask him in, of course,'' she said smoothly, reaching out a hand to make sure he didn't escape. ''What is your name?'' she asked him quickly.

''Mitch. Mitch Harper,'' he said, looking back longingly at his car.

''Nice to meet you, Mitch.'' Getting a good grip on his arm, she turned and called out, ''Look, everybody. It's Hailey's friend, Mitch. Let's make him feel at home.''

Peering into the house, Mitch saw nothing but a sea of female faces and his heart sank.

''Hi, Mitch,'' a short redhead said, freeing a chair for him. ''Sit here. You're just in time to play Baby Bottle Bingo with us.''

He turned as if to make a run for it, but Cami was too quick for him. She led him to the chair and made sure he was securely seated, then turned away to talk to Sara.

"Rafe is just pulling up outside," she noted, her eyes bright. "I'll grab him and head for the airport. I only hope we can catch her in time."

"Hurry," Sara whispered, hugging her. "It doesn't look to me like he'll last too long in this environment. Too many women around. Some men just wilt, you know."

Cami nodded. "I know Rafe would be out of here like a shot. Okay. We'll go as fast as we can." She grinned at her friend. "At least I've got my own private cop along. That ought to help. See you!"

Sara watched her go, then turned back to Mitch, who was looking as uncomfortable as a bear at a ballet.

"Where is Hailey?" he asked her, half-rising out of his chair, only to be knocked back down as the redhead thrust a bingo card in his lap.

"She's...uh...she's coming down in just a minute. We've sent for her. She ought to be here anytime now." And she smiled at him reassuringly and hoped he didn't notice that her fingers were crossed behind her back. "Would you like some punch?"

He got some punch, whether he wanted it or not, along with a thick slice of cake, a cup of frosted nuts, and a goblet of green sherbet.

"Look, you've got bingo!" the redhead who'd been helping him juggle all those things and keep up with his card called out.

"Mitch has bingo. He gets the prize."

Everyone was talking at once. He looked around the room and found a dozen pairs of eyes fixed on him, each with a loving, mothering look. He could just imagine women leaning together, sighing and saying, "Oh, isn't it sweet? He's come all this way to find Hailey." This was a bit much for a man who liked to remain anonymous. He was beginning to itch all over.

"You won. Here's your prize."

Someone handed him a stuffed flamingo that said "Pretty baby" when you squeezed it. Just what he'd always wanted. Now he had so many things weighing him down, he couldn't get up if he wanted to. He looked around the room again, hoping against hope to catch sight of Hailey.

"She's coming," Sara called out, nodding at him. "Any minute now."

Mitch frowned. He was beginning to lose faith in her sense of time. They played another round of bingo, but his heart wasn't in it, and when the redhead won, he took it as a chance to make his move. Leaving his things behind, he slipped out of the chair and made a beeline for the front door, ignoring the chorus of women's voices calling him back.

"Hey, wait a minute," Sara called to him, coming up fast with the flamingo in her arms. "You can't leave yet. She's coming."

He looked back at the pretty woman and shook his head. "She obviously doesn't want to see me," he said, his voice husky. "I'm not going to force myself on her. And anyway, I can't take any more rounds of bingo. You'll just have to excuse me."

"But we're about to open the presents."

"I didn't bring one." Another goof. He was a fish out of water. He had to get away from here.

"You didn't have any cake." She was getting desperate now.

"Yes, I did," he said firmly. He was fed up and she could see that it was no use to beg further.

Sadly she handed him the flamingo. "Well, if you must go."

He took the pink bird and looked at it quizzically. "Look, I really have to leave. Tell Hailey…" His blue eyes looked so dark and hopeless, it broke her heart. "Just tell her I wish her the best and…"

A rental car came barreling around the corner and slid to a stop in front of the house with a screech that could have peeled the skin off a turkey.

"Mitch!" Hailey cried. She flung open the door and almost fell out of the car into the snow in her hurry. "Mitch, wait!"

She came flying toward him, her blond hair whipping behind her, a fur collar framing her face. Watching her, his heart filled with something hot and he had to reach out and put a hand on the railing to steady himself.

"Hi there," he said in a hearty voice meant to throw up a quick defense. He shifted the flamingo from one hand to the other and then tucked it under his arm. "So there you are."

Sara heard the tone and bit her lip, fading back into the house so as to give them some time alone. She shook her head as she went, but she could hardly suppress a smile.

Hailey, meanwhile, stopped just short of where he stood, hesitating. She'd been about to throw herself into his arms, but he was standing so straight, looking so closed, she realized he might not be here for the reason she'd assumed.

"Hi," she said, looking at him doubtfully. "Yes, here I am."

"Uh..." He paused. "I was in town and I just stopped by to see if you were okay."

She nodded and tried to read his mind. "I'm fine. How about you?" She added a bright smile.

"Me? I'm doing great. Everything worked out okay, didn't it?"

He stared down at her, unable to think of anything to add, and she looked up at him, her smile gradually melting into a frown of uncertainty.

He shifted his weight and looked toward his car. "Yeah...well...I think I'll go now," he said.

A flash of fire flared in Hailey eyes. This was just too much. "No," she said firmly, and stood with her hands on her hips, right in his way.

He looked at her, surprised. "No?" he echoed.

"No." She shook her head and thrust out her lower lip. "You didn't come all the way back just to say hello."

He swallowed and winced as he heard laughter coming from the party behind him. "I might have," he noted wistfully.

"But you didn't."

He glanced at her and then away. "I just wanted to make sure you were okay," he muttered.

"No," she said again.

He glared at her. "Why do you keep saying no?"

Her green gaze held his. "Because that's still not why you came."

His drew his brows together. "How the hell do you know why I came?" he demanded.

Her heart was beating so quickly she was afraid she might pass out. But she had to do this. If she didn't do this now, she would never forgive herself.

"I know why you came, because... because I know why I was about to go looking for you in California."

His eyes widened. "You were what?"

"That's where I was, at the airport buying a ticket for L.A. I wanted to see you."

"You can't go back to California." His frown was furious. "It's not safe for you yet."

She shook her head. "I didn't care about that. I had to see you."

He took her in, all of her, standing there in Sara's front yard with the snow all around them and the sky so blue behind, and something was surging through him. She'd been ready to risk danger to come to him. That was a switch. He was the one who was always taking care of others, and here she'd been ready to give everything up for him. At least, that was what he thought she meant when she said she had to see him. But just to be sure, he asked, "Oh, yeah? And why was that?"

She took a deep breath. This was it. The big spin. Everything was riding on this one. If she lost, she would be devastated. But if she won . . .

"Because I love you."

She said it loud and clear, and she looked him straight in the eye when she said it.

He blinked. He wasn't sure he'd heard right. "What?" he said.

She stared at him, then threw herself at him. "You heard me!" she cried, grabbing his jacket with both hands. "Don't you dare make me say it again until you . . ."

He was laughing. He didn't know why, but suddenly this was all so funny. "Until I what?" he teased, his heart so light it might have floated out of his body.

"Until you tell me how you feel," she insisted, searching his blue eyes.

He'd never said it before, not to anyone. His mouth tried to form the words, but it wasn't easy.

"I . . . I love you," he said at last, and she cried out and threw her arms around his neck.

It was going to be okay. He wasn't like all the rest. He'd come back. And now he'd admitted that he loved her. But something was jutting into her rib cage.

"Ouch," she said, drawing back and rubbing the wounded area. "What is that you're holding?"

"A flamingo," he said ruefully, holding it out. "Do you want it?"

"Is it for me?" she asked, slightly bewildered.

"Not exactly. I won it at bingo. In there." He gestured with his head toward where all the laughter was coming from.

She looked at him and laughed. "You participated in the shower?" she asked, delighted.

He made a face. "Yes. And I won't go back there. Don't try to make me."

She was in his arms again, this time making way for the large pink bird. "I wouldn't dream of it," she said, gazing up into his handsome face and thinking she was too lucky to believe.

He held her nicely enough, and kissed her, too, but his mind was still on the horrors of the shower. "Promise me you won't have one of these things when we have our babies," he said, nibbling at her chin line.

She stared up at him, her mouth gaping. "Our babies? Are we having some of those?"

"I guess so." He shrugged. "Isn't that what usually happens after you get married?"

"Yes," she said breathlessly, nodding very quickly and deciding on the spur of the moment not to bring up the fact that he hadn't asked her yet. "Oh, yes!"

But he wasn't completely oblivious. Leaning down, he dropped a warm kiss on her lips and whispered, "Will you? Marry me, I mean."

She nodded happily. "As long as you're sure."

"No problem. I'm sure."

"Then so am I. And the answer is yes!" She laughed, snuggling cozily against his wide chest. "Remember that song we danced to the night we met, 'Cowboys Never Fall in Love'? Do you still believe it?"

He dropped a kiss on her neck and another behind her ear. "That song is full of lies," he murmured.

She craned her head to look at him. "Are you sure?"

"I know it," he declared happily, and then added in an echo of what he'd said that night, "I've lived it."

She smiled and gazed into his eyes, her own filling with tears of joy. "I love you," she told him huskily.

"Good. Then it's settled. We're going to live happily ever after."

"Okay," she agreed, letting him lead her away from the house. "Sounds good to me."

A cheer rose from the shower. Something good must have happened. But the timing was right, and Mitch swung Hailey around so they both could take a bow, facing the house.

"Here, have a flamingo," Mitch said, perching the bird atop the mailbox.

And they walked off arm in arm, forgetting all about the rented car, too engrossed in each other to remember where they were, making lacy patterns in the snow, and falling forever in love.

*   *   *   *   *

Don't miss BABIES BY THE BUSLOAD,
the third book in Raye Morgan's exciting series,
THE BABY SHOWER, *coming this September,*
only from Silhouette Desire!

The first book in the exciting new
Fortune's Children series is

HIRED HUSBAND

by *New York Times* bestselling writer
Rebecca Brandewyne

Beginning in July 1996
Only from Silhouette Books

Here's an exciting sneak preview....

Minneapolis, Minnesota

As Caroline Fortune wheeled her dark blue Volvo into the underground parking lot of the towering, glass-and-steel structure that housed the global headquarters of Fortune Cosmetics, she glanced anxiously at her gold Piaget wristwatch. An accident on the snowy freeway had caused rush-hour traffic to be a nightmare this morning. As a result, she was running late for her 9:00 a.m. meeting—and if there was one thing her grandmother, Kate Winfield Fortune, simply couldn't abide, it was slack, unprofessional behavior on the job. And lateness was the sign of a sloppy, disorganized schedule.

Involuntarily, Caroline shuddered at the thought of her grandmother's infamous wrath being unleashed upon her. The stern rebuke would be precise, apropos, scathing and delivered with coolly raised, condemnatory eyebrows and in icy tones of haughty grandeur that had in the past reduced many an executive—even the male ones—at Fortune Cosmetics not only to obsequious apologies, but even to tears. Caroline had seen it happen on more than one occasion, although, much to her gratitude and relief, she herself was seldom a target of her grandmother's anger. And she wouldn't be this morning, either, not if she could help it. That would be a disastrous way to start out the new year.

Grabbing her Louis Vuitton totebag and her black leather portfolio from the front passenger seat, Caroline stepped gracefully from the Volvo and slammed the door. The heels of her Maud Frizon pumps clicked briskly on the concrete floor as she hurried toward the bank of elevators that would take her up into the skyscraper owned by her family. As the elevator doors slid open, she rushed down the long, plushly carpeted corridors of one of the hushed upper floors toward the conference room.

By now Caroline had her portfolio open and was leafing through it as she hastened along, reviewing her notes she had prepared for her presentation. So she didn't see Dr. Nicolai Valkov until she literally ran right into him. Like her, he had his head bent over his own portfolio, not watching where he was going. As the two of them collided, both their portfolios and the papers inside went flying. At the unexpected impact, Caroline lost her balance, stumbled, and would have fallen had not Nick's strong, sure hands abruptly shot out, grabbing hold of her and pulling her to him to steady her. She gasped, startled and stricken, as she came up hard against his broad chest, lean hips and corded thighs, her face just inches from his own—as though they were lovers about to kiss.

Caroline had never been so close to Nick Valkov before, and, in that instant, she was acutely aware of him—not just as a fellow employee of Fortune Cosmetics but also as a man. Of how tall and ruggedly handsome he was, dressed in an elegant, pin-striped black suit cut in the European fashion, a crisp white shirt, a foulard tie and a pair of Cole Haan loafers. Of how dark his thick, glossy hair and his deep-set eyes framed by raven-wing brows were so dark that they were almost black, despite the bright, fluorescent lights that blazed overhead. Of the whiteness of his straight teeth against his bronzed skin as a brazen, mocking grin slowly curved his wide, sensual mouth.

"Actually, I *was* hoping for a sweet roll this morning—but I daresay you would prove even tastier, Ms. Fortune," Nick drawled impertinently, his low, silky voice tinged with a faint accent born of the fact that Russian, not English, was his native language.

At his words, Caroline flushed painfully, embarrassed and annoyed. If there was one person she always attempted to avoid at Fortune Cosmetics, it was Nick Valkov. Following the breakup of the Soviet Union, he had emigrated to the United States, where her grandmother had hired him to direct the company's research and development department. Since that time, Nick had constantly demonstrated marked, traditional, Old World tendencies that had led Caroline to believe he not only had no use for equal rights but also would actually have been more than happy to turn back the clock several centuries where females were concerned. She thought his remark was typical of his attitude toward women: insolent, arrogant and domineering. Really, the man was simply insufferable!

Caroline couldn't imagine what had ever prompted her grandmother to hire him—and at a highly generous salary, too—except that Nick Valkov was considered one of the foremost chemists anywhere on the planet. Deep down inside Caroline knew that no matter how he behaved, Fortune Cosmetics was extremely lucky to have him. Still, that didn't give him the right to manhandle and insult her!

"I assure you that you would find me more bitter than a cup of the strongest black coffee, Dr. Valkov," she insisted, attempting without success to free her trembling body from his steely grip, while he continued to hold her so near that she could feel his heart beating steadily in his chest—and knew he must be equally able to feel the erratic hammering of her own.

"Oh, I'm willing to wager there's more sugar and cream to you than you let on, Ms. Fortune." To her utter mortification and outrage, she felt one of Nick's hands slide insidiously up her back and nape to her luxuriant mass of sable hair, done up in a stylish French twist.

"You know so much about fashion," he murmured, eyeing her assessingly, pointedly ignoring her indignation and efforts to escape from him. "So why do you always wear your hair like this... so tightly wrapped and severe? I've never seen it down. Still, that's the way it needs to be worn, you know...soft, loose, tangled about your face. As it is, your hair fairly cries out for a man to take the pins from it, so he can see how long it is. Does it fall past your shoulders?" He quirked one eyebrow inquisitively, a mocking half smile still twisting his lips, letting her know he was enjoying her obvious discomfiture. "You aren't going to tell me, are you? What a pity. Because my guess is that it does—and I'd like to know if I'm right. And these glasses." He indicated the large, square, tortoiseshell frames perched on her slender, classic nose. "I think you use them to hide behind more than you do to see. I'll bet you don't actually even need them at all."

Caroline felt the blush that had yet to leave her cheeks deepen, its heat seeming to spread throughout her entire quivering body. Damn the man! Why must he be so infuriatingly perceptive?

Because everything that Nick suspected was true.

*   *   *   *   *

To read more, don't miss
HIRED HUSBAND
by Rebecca Brandewyne,
Book One in the new
FORTUNE'S CHILDREN series,
beginning this month and available only from
Silhouette Books!

A Funny Thing Happened on the Way to the Baby Shower...

When four college friends reunite to celebrate the arrival of one bouncing baby, they find four would-be grooms on the way!

Don't miss a single, sexy tale in

RAYE MORGAN'S

Only in

BABY DREAMS
in May '96 (SD #997)

A GIFT FOR BABY
in July '96 (SD #1010)

BABIES BY THE BUSLOAD
in September '96 (SD #1022)

And look for

INSTANT DAD, WILL TRAIN
in November '96

Only from

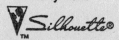

RMBS

Silhouette's recipe for a sizzling summer:

* Take the best-looking cowboy in South Dakota
* Mix in a brilliant bachelor
* Add a sexy, mysterious sheikh
* Combine their stories into one collection and you've got one sensational super-hot read!

Summer Sizzlers

MEN OF *Summer*

Three short stories by these favorite authors:

Kathleen Eagle
Joan Hohl
Barbara Faith

Available this July wherever
Silhouette books are sold.

Look us up on-line at: http://www.romance.net

Silhouette®

™

SS96

Who can resist a Texan...or a Calloway?

This September, award-winning author
ANNETTE BROADRICK
returns to Texas, with a brand-new
story about the Calloways...

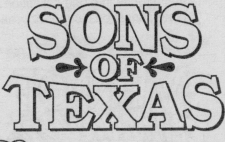

SONS
OF
TEXAS

Rogues and Ranchers

CLINT: The brave leader. Used to keeping secrets.

CADE: The Lone Star Stud. Used to having women
fall at his feet...

MATT: The family guardian. Used to handling
trouble...

They must discover the identity of the mystery
woman with Calloway eyes—and uncover a
conspiracy that threatens their family....

Look for **SONS OF TEXAS:** Rogues and Ranchers
in September 1996!

Only from Silhouette...where passion lives.

FORTUNE'S Children™

New York Times Bestselling Author
REBECCA BRANDEWYNE

Launches a new twelve-book series—FORTUNE'S CHILDREN
beginning in July 1996 with Book One

Hired Husband

Caroline Fortune knew her marriage to Nick Valkov was in
name only. She would help save the family business, Nick
would get a green card, and a paper marriage would suit both
of them. Until Caroline could no longer deny the feelings Nick
stirred in her and the practical union turned passionate.

MEET THE FORTUNES—a family whose legacy is greater than
riches. Because where there's a will…there's a wedding!

Look for Book Two, *The Millionaire and the Cowgirl*,
by Lisa Jackson. Available in August 1996 wherever Silhouette
books are sold.

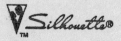